THE APARTMENT ON
CALLE URUGUAY

THE

APARTMENT

ON

CALLE URUGUAY

A Novel

Zachary Lazar

Catapult
New York

ISBN: 978-1-64622-111-0

Jacket design by Sarah Brody
Book design by Wah-Ming Chang

Library of Congress Control Number: 2021938317

Catapult
New York, NY
books.catapult.co

Printed in the United States of America
1 2 3 4 5 6 7 8 9 10

For Quntos KunQuest and Layla Roberts

I saw that under the mask of these half-humorous innuendoes, this old seaman, as an insulated Quakerish Nantucketer, was full of his insular prejudices, and rather distrustful of all aliens, unless they hailed from Cape Cod or the Vineyard.

"But what takes thee a-whaling? I want to know that before I think of shipping ye."

"Well, sir, I want to see what whaling is. I want to see the world."

"Want to see what whaling is, eh? Have ye clapped eye on Captain Ahab?"

"Who is Captain Ahab, sir?"

"Aye, aye, I thought so. Captain Ahab is the Captain of this ship."

HERMAN MELVILLE
from *Moby-Dick*

THE APARTMENT ON
CALLE URUGUAY

1

magine watching the raw footage of every minute of your life—what you were seeing, hearing, feeling, thinking, including moments you barely noticed or didn't notice at all—then imagine entering that stream at random and trying to recognize where you were, what was happening. Would what had seemed important still seem important in the same way? Would what had seemed trivial, or had never even registered, seem rich with interest now that you were viewing it so close up and with such urgency? The flash of life from dead matter, mineral to plant, plant to animal, animal to human with mind and soul or at least the idea of mind and soul—there were all these miracles presenting themselves every second of our lives and then there was the destructiveness of that summer, that year, the years to follow.

I hadn't seen my neighbor Diana very much lately—she

was busy with work as she usually was—but that evening both of us happened to have had a free moment at the same time. I had just gotten off the phone with a curator who wanted to ask me a few questions about Malika, and it was confusing, as if for a moment Malika were still alive, and I was in this kind of a fog when I wandered down the path, past the house Diana rented part of, toward the pond. The house she rented in was a yellow bungalow with reclaimed junk in the front yard, old desks and chairs and stereo consoles that her new boyfriend Sebastian seemed to be making a habit of refinishing in a slow, mostly imperceptible way. Diana was my age, late forties or early fifties, someone who had been through a lot (I knew too much about her from being her next-door neighbor), and since the advent of Sebastian, she had bloomed into some version of who she'd probably been a long time ago. Sebastian was maybe twenty years younger, with a muscular build and kinky blond hair, and he went around shirtless, like a TV star from the '70s. He'd told me once how much he liked older women, the character in their faces. I didn't know where he was that afternoon, it was just Diana, who was down at the dock when I got there, hoisting herself up onto the planks after a swim, a tattoo of a cresting wave on her belly just above the waistline.

"The damn geese," she said. "All this shit on the dock. I don't know what to do about it."

She shook water out of her hair, then wrapped herself in an old beach towel the color of split pea soup.

"Not really my skill set," I said. "How was the sailing yesterday?"

"Fine. Windy. Nothing great. I don't weigh much, so I'm not much good in the wind."

"I thought wind was kind of the point."

"Kind of. Kind of sort of."

Her gaze was suggestive sometimes, flirty, Sebastian notwithstanding, but there was hostility buried in it that I don't think she thought I could see and maybe couldn't see herself. She always thought I came from Brooklyn, which I guessed had something to do with the color of my skin. This kind of friction was worse now, since the election that fall, though I doubted Diana voted that way, if she voted at all, unless she did, smiling suggestively at me as she had before.

"August," I said.

"We're going to grill tonight, if you want to come by."

"You and Sebastian."

"And some of his friends. They're all coming from the city. He's on his way back now, he just finished a job."

"I'll try to stop by."

"Well, keep it in mind."

"Thank you."

"You going in?"

"Yeah, right now."

The pond was more than two miles across—I'd heard people say it looked like New Hampshire or Vermont, which were places I had never stayed in long enough to actually see. I think what they meant was the pond was surrounded by pine trees—very thick in the distance—as well as deciduous ones—oaks and maples and tupelos. Diana feared the pond was dying and that one day it would truly die, an algal bloom would kill all the fish—the egrets had already stopped roosting in the trees in the evenings—but for now there were still perch and even some bass, despite the chemicals leaching in from people's lawns, and in at least this diminished sense the pond survived.

I dove straight off the dock, reaching forward and hitting the water at just the right angle, and swam underwater for as long as I could. It was warm, though still cooler than the air, and swimming through it felt purifying. When I came up, I was facing the deepest part of the pond and the nearest trees were very far away, and because there were no houses on that side, it was like I had traveled many miles (to Vermont, perhaps) instead of just swimming forty or fifty yards. The water was blue when you looked across it at the distant shore, but when you looked up close it was striated with white and gray waveforms that moved and regenerated endlessly. I thought about the curator who had called about Malika earlier. As I got older, I had more, not less, trouble locating myself in the changes I'd gone through—maybe everyone felt that way at my age, though perhaps they didn't feel that the changes were so senseless. The curator was writing descriptive text about an artist's book Malika had made called *Darkadia*, after a fictional island nation, part Caribbean, part New York City, that constituted the book's purported "subject." I saw now that it was really Malika's outsider vision of Manhattan, that she was trying to see the city around her from an estranged perspective that might reflect her own alienation and fear, but it also reminded me of the New York I had first encountered when I came here from Israel when I was ten (my mother and I started off in the Village, before giving up and moving, yes, to Brooklyn, then Queens). I told the curator that back then Malika and many other people we knew felt a violent culmination coming, not another September 11 but something domestic aroused or revitalized by September 11 that would pull everything apart. Malika had talked about her project as a kind of "negative fantasy," an imagined apocalypse in place of the endless cycle of violence and amnesia that was America's actual history. It was a release, in other words, albeit a negative one.

I had lost the thread of this swim. I realized I had been treading water for quite some time now without even being aware of it, without seeing anything around me, and for reasons I didn't really understand. I looked back at the dock and it was still there, now empty, Diana gone. The trees were barely moving in the light breeze, and the sky above was piled with billowing clouds, white and gilded at the edges. I kept swimming. The tupelos' leaves had already turned color, red against the deep green of the thick forest behind them. When I turned around, the blue water of the pond and the hazy trees in the background were like icons of themselves.

Malika's brother Jesse had tried to call me while I was at the pond—I knew now why I'd become upset while I was swimming. It was not the curator, or even Malika's memory, but the premonition of the missed call. The female robot had left a voice mail and my phone had transcribed the message, starting somewhere in the middle:

seven if you would like to permanently block your number from receiving calls from this facility press six for balance and rate quotes press one to accept charges press two to refuse charges press seven if you would like to permanently block your number from receiving calls from this facility press—

I hadn't seen Jesse since last Christmas—we became close only after Malika's death, or because of it. He had grown a new beard, which he kept neatly trimmed, thanks to a friendship he'd made with the inmate barber. The facility's walls were two-toned, the lower third, because it got dinged the most, darker, to spare the paint from showing wear and tear. We sat in the visiting shed and made jokes and gossiped—Jesse was always in good spirits when I came—and both of us had sandwiches and a soda. The glint of hope now was that he had applied for clemency that spring. The glint of despair was that he'd applied two years ago, we had gone through the whole process, and he'd been denied, and so he was reluctant now to go through that all over again. I couldn't just call him back now—that was the problem—so I sent him an email. I told him about coming across Diana down at the dock in her bikini, then the vexed thoughts about Malika while I swam in the pond. I told him about the curator who had called. It always felt like I was writing from another world, which I was.

Don't lose sight of what you can't see, I closed, a paraphrase of something Jesse himself had said to me once.

I went out to my backyard, looking at the trees until I began to see them. There was a wooded lot beyond mine, all oaks, and I had lived with them for a while now, they had never failed me. Even when I heard the cars on the main road, I could still take something from how the trees' leaves moved or didn't move according to the air. The largest one grew five stories high, its branches spread out like predatory arms, all of its leaves toothed like something primeval. Behind me was a modest lawn and behind that a half circle of daylilies that I'd inherited from the previous owner. I didn't know what a daylily was until I bought the house. A daylily's flowers bloom and die in one day.

The house where Ana was staying was across the giant oak

trees from me. I'd been seeing Ana for about three months then.

There was a place I liked to buy fish, and I took Ana there that evening after she got back from work and changed her clothes. The fish shop was a shack built on the edge of an inlet where the boats would dock and unload their catch. From the parking lot, you could see the inlet itself, silver beneath the sky, fringed with reeds, and you could smell the briny air and hear the seagulls flying toward the abandoned coast guard station down the road. Inside, there were rubber mats on the water-drenched floor where Ana and I stood. All along the wall beside us lay whole fish arrayed on ice—silver, pink, gray, yellow—their dead eyes black and rimmed with green. We kept touching each other, even in the fish shop. She wore what I now knew was called a huipil, embroidered with large pink roses on a black ground. Hers was a modern version, which went well with her cutoff jeans, the loose threads coming down in strands on her thighs. I felt us glaring there in the line, the counterwoman working the register before iced vats of mussels, clams, cockles, steamers, crabs. Men in aprons and high rubber boots worked at the cutting tables and sinks, filleting fish with their knives, and I felt our conspicuousness modulating my voice into something mesmerizingly calm, as I asked the woman what had come in fresh today. I had made rice at home. They sold bok choi, so I bought some bok choi. They bagged the scallops and filleted the fish and packed it all in ice and we walked back outside to my truck.

"Ceviche," I said. "They have that in Mexico, but what about sushi? I'm not trying to sound ignorant."

"There's sushi everywhere."

"There's tacos here but they're not really tacos. What I mean, is the sushi there any good?"

"I don't know. Compared to what? There's sushi everywhere in the world."

"Your friend is still coming out next week. Jack?"

She looked out the window, not answering, her hand still entwined in mine. "How can you not know him? He's your neighbor."

"Does he like sushi?"

"You're being stupid."

I'd been reading the Bible that summer, which I do from time to time, and I'd just gotten to a part in the book of Exodus where Moses, having fled Egypt, marries a wife who knows nothing about his past and gives birth to a son, Gershom, which means "stranger in a strange land." This was how I often felt that summer with Ana.

When we got back to my house, it smelled sour inside from the vinegar in the rice. Ana followed me into the kitchen, but there was nothing she could do to help, so I asked her to go put on some music. She connected her phone and used her streaming service to play something she liked, electronic, probably from Venezuela or Mexico but I had no idea. She was gone for a while and when she came back I could taste smoke on her lips from the joint she'd lit up. She looked up at me and my eyes moved from her eyes to her fingertips and back. I felt her body through the huipil, her leanness not as hard and articulated as Malika's had been. I pressed my fingers to the vertebrae just above her waist, then smoothed my hands down over her ass to her thighs, which were bare beneath the cutoffs. The huipil was from Mexico but she was from Venezuela. In four weeks, she was returning to Mexico City, where she and most of her family had resettled several years ago after fleeing Caracas. If you walked through my backyard into the woods, you could pick up a hiking trail that went for miles through a nature preserve, all the way to the bay, but first you had to walk across a few people's lawns, and that was how I first came across Ana, walking through these other people's properties, which always made me feel a little furtive, even at that time of year when there was hardly anyone around. It was May, still ugly out, damp and cold, and a neighbor's dog, Chloe, started barking when I saw Ana and she saw me. She wore a fur-trimmed coat that went down to her knees, not looking at me but at Chloe, who continued to bark and was now rushing up on her. Despite her small stature, Ana had a strong presence—I saw that immediately in the way she stood with her hips a little forward, clapping her gloved hands and then reaching toward Chloe, beckoning, not scared. I introduced myself and told her I lived back through the woods. The trunks of the trees were soaked black with the previous night's rain, the first grass coming up through the road's sandy clay. She was standing next to a pile of old records and books that she must have cleared out of the house. I offered to get my truck and take it up to the dump for her.

"Jack said they'd come pick it up," she told me. "He said I should just leave it there."

"Who?"

"Jack, your neighbor. My friend. You don't know him?"

"No. I don't think so."

I knew almost no one in the neighborhood, apart from Diana and her landlord.

She had gone solemn in the kitchen now—I had taken her hair out of the clip, and it hung on either side of her face and for some reason that made her look sad or vaguely lost. There was something regressive about the attraction between us, I thought. Sometimes we spent so much time together that we didn't sleep or eat. It wasn't that we were fucking all the time, a lot of it was just me listening to her talk. I would try to put together something closer to an actual picture of her, but I'd get distracted by a new piece of information, then miss the next one while I was trying to synthesize it all. She liked to talk and I liked to listen to her voice. I had made abstract paintings and I liked certain forms of jazz, and this was something like that. I left the fish and the knife on the counter and we went into the bedroom.

She was naming places she'd been: India, Thailand, China, Brazil, the list so long that she trailed off and I asked her to tell me one thing about each of the places at random. She said that in India there was a cave on an island off Mumbai where there was an image of Shiva carved out of stone, his three faces—creator, preserver, destroyer—what they used to call "sublime," not beautiful, something beyond that. She had met some friends of friends in India, she said, one of whom turned out to be the son of the Maharajah of Jodhpur, whose house was a palace with gates tall enough for elephants to pass through, with an endless lawn where fires burned in two rows of iron bowls (I remember this story as a set of images, not words—I don't remember what Ana's actual words were). Before that night at the son of the Maharajah's palace, she told me, she had visited a museum in another palace—a room with nothing in it but baby cradles, a room with just mirrors, a room full of antique photographs of the old royal families. One of them was a portrait of a princess from Jodhpur who was living in Paris when the Nazis arrived. I lay there picturing this princess with her hair uncovered, in a mink coat, in soft-focus black and white. Some of this princess's closest friends were Jews, Ana said—this was all told in the wall text by the photograph—and she bartered her jewels to help them escape to the United States, but the plan was discovered by the Gestapo, and they deported the princess to Germany. At the son of the Maharajah's palace, Ana said, with the fires burning in those iron bowls, white wine from France in her glass, she kept thinking about that princess from Jodhpur, who eventually died in a concentration camp. What she and her family had lost in Venezuela seemed arrayed before her in that palace garden, like that museum in the other palace with its room full of baby carriages, its room full of mirrors, the photograph of the princess from Jodhpur in the room full of antique photographs. I thought of Malika watching over us as Ana told me this story, and when I saw us through Malika's eyes I could hardly stand my sense of falseness. I still felt that way after all this time unless I was alone.

"These are just memories," Ana said. "But you don't seem like you even have any memories. You're just sort of there."

"I never really felt right about traveling. It felt like going to a zoo, you were gaping, or trying to understand things you had no idea about. It felt almost like stealing to me."

"I thought the whole point of life was to try to understand things you had no idea about."

"I'm just talking about myself."

"I'm not even sure what that means anymore."

"As in, who am I?"

"Yes. Something like that."

"I didn't know much about Venezuela until I met you. I mean, I knew some things from the news—the riots, the food shortages—but I didn't really follow it. I followed Syria, Iraq. Libya. The Ukraine."

"And then you saw me one day in front of Jack's house."

"Jack. Who I don't even know."

She pulled closer to me. I kept seeing us through Malika's eyes, then pushing away that thought—I remembered Diana on the dock, Sebastian's furniture on the lawn, the sushi Ana and I had left mostly uneaten, having barely touched it after I'd spent so much time finally preparing it, after our first trip to this bedroom, standing in the kitchen in just a pair of shorts, Ana sitting at the table, smoking the rest of her joint.

I thought of an image I'd seen of Caracas, recognizable only by a Venezuelan flag in the background, small fires burning in the street while a young man in a gas mask got ready to throw a Molotov cocktail.

2

The weekend her friend Jack came to stay with her was the weekend of the white supremacist rally in Charlottesville. There were a lot of things I was trying not to think about that Saturday when I went to see my friend Jerome, who lived a few miles south, and he must have felt the same, we could see something in each other's eyes. I remembered the sushi I'd made for me and Ana, raw red tuna, fish eggs, the pale green of the wasabi, the nori darker, almost black. Jerome told me he had burned himself slightly all along the inside of his arm and the side of his chest the other day while using a TIG welder. He mimed the injury for me now and made a look of bewildered acceptance, his face surprisingly old, even showing wrinkles at the corners of his eyes—we were both getting older. With a TIG welder, you had to hold the electrode steady at the correct angle, melting the metal surface into a tiny puddle in a straight line while adding fill with your other hand, and you had to do it while looking through a thick glass shield that made it hard to see, which meant you had to do it almost by memory or feel. I told Jerome about when I had learned how to use one of those things, and how one of the other students set himself on fire and we all just stood there facing forward with our heat shields over our faces, until finally we heard him screaming.

"Man, I barely knew what happened until later that night," Jerome said. "I went to take a shower and I'm like, what the fuck."

"Exfoliated."

"Yeah, right. Like a spa treatment. Right there in my garage."

We were in his living room, where on the TV commentators spoke over images from the previous night's rally. The governor of Virginia had declared martial law, but crowds remained near the newly renamed Emancipation Square, where the Robert E. Lee statue still stood. The symbols of whiteness had become the tiki torch and the polo shirt, referencing Polynesia and a sport from India (the burning cross and the white hood and sheet only alluded to, gentrified so much that the commentators didn't seem to even see them). It put Jerome in mind of a couple whose trees he took care of, an old man and his much younger wife, who still thought of herself as an actress, he said. The man had told Jerome once he was a vegetarian—it had to do with the Holocaust, the idea of meat reminding him of images he'd seen of bodies tossed into the mass graves at Auschwitz. He was a Jew from South Africa who'd lived through apartheid and then come to work on Wall Street, where he made enough money to afford a wife thirty years younger than he was. Now she had to listen to him as he died of cancer, Jerome said, compulsively following the news on TV, addicted to it. Yesterday Jerome had seen them arguing through the sliding glass doors as he trimmed their cypress trees, a beautiful woman with her hand on her hip, arm cocked.

"He came all the way from South Africa because he couldn't stand the politics," he said.

"He came here."

"Haha. Right."

"I didn't know you were supposed to prune cypress trees in the summer. You have an interesting life, Jerome, somebody should make a movie."

"Sort of like *Being There*."

"Okay, so you're Jesus now."

"Yeah, that's one interpretation. Either that or it's saying Jesus is just some autistic gardener."

He offered me some eggs from his laying hens in the backyard and I followed him into the kitchen, where he kept them in cartons on the counter rather than in the refrigerator. We used to hunt together. I was good at it until one day my shot didn't kill the deer, just sent it charging off into the woods, its face blown off, and I never could find it to put it out of its misery. I stopped hunting after that. I stopped eating meat. If I couldn't imagine killing it myself, I wasn't going to eat it—I was a little like the man from South Africa in that way. The eggs from Jerome's hens were not like eggs in stores, they had dark orange yolks that looked so rich you wanted to taste them raw. I didn't eat meat, but I still ate eggs. I was already thinking about sharing some of them with Ana when the weekend was over, still trying to convince myself that I didn't care that she was with her friend Jack right now, and I was having these daydreams when Jerome and I heard the sounds from the television in the living room and we went back in to see what happened.

Screams were coming from a crowd of counterprotesters who were massed near a pedestrian mall dressed in shorts and T-shirts, some of them carrying flags. A black car had just sped right into them, smashing into another car, then reversing so fast it was almost more shocking than the crash itself. Some people sprinted toward the tangle of bodies and metal, others staggered away. It kept happening in replays, the black Dodge Challenger trailing two streamers of debris from its front bumper, its windshield shattered, rocketing back and forth into the crowd.

Jerome wouldn't look at me, his head bowed, hands at his sides, then he barely raised the one that hung waist-level nearest me and went back into the kitchen. It felt as if a war had started, the one Malika had always feared. The South African man, *Being There*—I saw now that this banter was not so much Jerome's effort to bring us closer as friends but a way to fend off the rage we could only partly share, the gulf whose seriousness now stared at me.

There used to be slavery here in New York—twenty percent of this county had once been slaves. Some of them had been my friend Jerome's ancestors. He'd grown up on the Indian reservation to the west of town and he kept a wind catcher hanging from the rearview mirror of his truck, embracing another part of his ancestry, which went back in this country about ten thousand years.

I walked down to the main road to get my mail and saw Diana and Sebastian out on the front lawn, but I didn't want to deal with them so I averted my eyes and kept moving, which made me feel eccentric. I saw myself standing with a black hood over my head, electrodes at my fingertips, while my neighbors smiled with thumbs up as at Abu Ghraib. The president's face and voice filled me with this kind of madness, though it was not really madness. When I came back with the mail, which was only flyers and bills, I had no choice but to look directly at Diana and Sebastian, who I now saw were cleaning fish, hunched over in the grass next to the old wooden furniture Sebastian was refinishing. The boughs of the trees above me were like dark arms, the leaves shimmering in the gold light of the sky. I saluted Diana and Sebastian, then turned and went inside my house. Perhaps they hadn't heard the news from Charlottesville or perhaps the most sensible thing possible on a day like this was to go fishing. I didn't know.

I spoke to Jesse, Malika's brother, on the phone that afternoon. The president had made a speech that didn't mention the murdered young woman, but tacitly blamed her and her fellow protesters for her death. Already people had forgotten the young white man who, two years ago, had murdered those nine worshippers in the Emanuel AME church in Charleston in the name of the Lost Cause. They wanted to forget about those murders but to remember the beautiful equestrian statues cast in bronze.

"The president," Jesse said. "What do you say to people about that, up there?"

"It depends who I'm talking to," I said. "Why we're talking."

"I guess Kanye's up there. Jay-Z and Beyoncé."

"You need to put down the *In Touch* magazines."

"You ain't say shit to people up there, in other words."

"The point of moving here: not saying shit to people. Not hearing the shit I had to say to them. A win-win."

"I'm just glad they don't have TV in this dorm. Just in the

common area. They want to kill us, all of us. It's like 9/11, they had us on lockdown, and a rumor started spreading that the next phase was they were going to execute us all. All us lifers. It didn't sound like a crazy rumor to me. Not crazy at all. White people panicking."

"It's an ugly day."

"Whatever it is, I need to get some distance from it."

He'd gotten a new hearing—that was why he'd tried to call me the other day. In an email, he'd told me about it and that he wasn't getting his hopes up, but I'd be getting a letter from the division of pardon and parole reminding me of the details about how to attend. The letter still hadn't arrived.

"November," I said.

"I'm not really thinking about it."

"Sounds familiar. I mean, it sounds like me. Maybe you can come visit up here when it's all over."

"You and Kanye tight, huh?"

"Something like that."

"Man, I been checking out—"

His sentence was cut off by a simulated voice message telling us our time was up.

"The Bible. Had not picked that up in a while."

"The Bible."

"Here's the story of why we were slaves in Egypt, it starts with the dawn of time—day splitting off from night, heaven from earth, Adam from Eve."

"Jay-Z from Beyoncé."

"Polarization. Everything's about schisms. Zeros and ones. The whole universe. The Bible, haha. It has it all."

"It's good news you got."

"Yeah. All right."

"I mean it. I'm glad you found God."

"Ha. Okay, I gotta go."

"I'll talk to you soon."

"Yeah, peace. Peace out."

"Okay. Soon."

There was an awkward little moment of silence, an unexpected second or two of extra time we failed to use before our connection finally broke off.

We'd been reading Baldwin together that summer, the essays proving timeless in the worst sense, as in they could have been written now. Baldwin's old house in the south of France had recently gone up for sale, the place where he'd found sanctuary, or at least somewhere he could live, not die. The driver of the Dodge Challenger had come all the way from Ohio, choked with wounded rage—Baldwin would not have been surprised that the woman he killed was white, like him, whatever "white" means. I never wanted to probe very far with Ana, accepting that her relationship with Jack was none of my business, that she and I had no claim on each other, but as I sat in my living room, no lamps on to mitigate the dimness, I kept thinking about that instead of thinking about Charlottesville and what it might have meant to her. Since May, she'd been helping a small local newspaper adjust to the "digital environment" after her journalism work in the city had dried up—she'd been trying New York, having never felt settled in Mexico—and her work clothes were expensive, skirts and tailored suits and silk blouses, worn with heels or flats that suggested a past very different from her present. I didn't know her, in other words. It didn't change anything for me that I didn't know her. When we first had sex, she asked if I had any special things I liked, and I liked this, but it also occurred to me that she was only there in the first place because I lived across the woods and it was convenient. There was a reason I'd retreated out here, I thought. I had lost some part of myself a long time ago, even before Malika died. I was lucky a friend of mine was investing back then, and I'd entrusted him with a chunk of my money, and things had gone well. I was lucky that his dead friend left this house in the turmoil of his estate and I was able to buy it. Later, I was lucky that the local college wanted my name, if not so much my actual person, on its faculty. I remembered the last time Jesse and I were talking in the visiting shed, someone had passed behind his chair and he stopped eating his sandwich for a moment. I couldn't even tell he was upset until he said so. Did people just do that in the world, he asked, walk behind your chair? I told him yeah, sometimes a person might even put his hand on the back of your chair, or even touch your shoulder as he passed by, and Jesse took that in as if I were telling him people outside walked around naked. He seemed more surprised than concerned. He told me he didn't know how he would handle that, if he ever got the chance to handle that.

I drove into the city, to my friend Lucien's place in East Harlem, away from what I'd seen on Jerome's TV. It had been years since I'd had a drink or used drugs but I was recognizing the dryness in my mouth, the consciousness of time bearing down on me. It was still light out when I got to the city. Coming toward me as I sat at a stop signal on 125th Street was a swarm of young men on bicycles, riding against the traffic. When the light changed and I was just starting up again, one of the kids veered out of control, picking up speed as he raised up on his back wheel, and almost hit the car in front of me. I was still taking this in when he brought his front wheel up even further and gracefully traced the edge of the car's windshield with something like a bullfighter's flourish, then came down headed toward me. We made eye contact and I thought of the car striking the crowd in Charlottesville. I was looking at the young man in concern and he was glaring at me with defiant craziness, until our gazes met and he saw that I was finally getting it, finally starting to smile, and he smiled too. I found a parking spot a few blocks up on 127th Street, where many of the storefront signs were in Spanish. It was August and the city was nearly empty. Back on 125th, a few food carts and street vendors selling belts and hair products vied with the new big-box chain stores. Lucien's building was a remnant of different times, half a block down from an indoor mall. He was in Europe, but I had a key—I stayed there sometimes, whether he was home or not—and I held the electronic fob to the door button and waited for the noise. The stairwell was dark and smelled like mildew. When I reached the second-floor landing, a slender young man sitting on the stairs peered up at me through black-framed eyeglasses, his gaze like some echo of that young man rising up on his bicycle, and I walked past him and let myself into Lucien's loft.

On the far wall was a brown drapery, like something from a child's playroom, decorated with red barns, yellow haystacks, pitchforks, cows. I drew it back to uncover a large TV monitor, flickering with an image of a theater, glittering stars hung from its ceiling on lengths of gold-colored filament. An arrangement of human bodies knelt forward on the stage with their heads on the floor, maybe twenty of them, naked, their skin painted gold. They suddenly rose up on their feet in warlike stances, becoming an army of tiny men and women wielding cloth-shrouded shields, some of them wearing necklaces made of animal bones. A strobe light began to muddle and attenuate their twistings, accentuating the ghostly incoherence of their shifts and leaps, and things began to move more and more slowly, farther and farther into the distance, and I began to lose my sense of where I was. It became clear that the dancers' shields were not shields at all but nets, triangular nets in the shape of sails, sails that caught the air as the dancers began to pace in their expanding circle, extending the sail-like nets before them in their hands. There was the feeling of drifting toward sleep at the wheel of a car, the road going by, lights flashing, half-asleep in the dark car, the road going by, lights flashing.

I closed the curtain.

I woke up the next morning in Lucien's vast open loft. I pissed and washed my face, then squeezed some of Lucien's toothpaste on my fingertip and did the best I could to clean my teeth. I saw myself in the mirror, spidery lines at the corners of my eyes, gray, almost white roots where my knotted hair emerged from the scalp. I still looked better than I wanted to, could still fool people and even myself with my appearance. I made some coffee in one of those small aluminum pots with two chambers separated by a screen. The studio part of Lucien's space was kind of a cabinet of curiosities. In addition to the TV monitor behind the barnyard curtain, there was a life-size skeleton draped with plastic-covered wires and electrodes, like dead hair or seaweed, with yet another TV monitor affixed to its rib cage. People might trace it to Haitian religion, the Guédé, I thought, or they might claim it was a parody of such art, or some statement about technology's relation to morbidity or eternity or just death, perhaps, but I knew Lucien was actually more interested in making paintings anyway. I thought of Malika's depictions of men in exaggerated hip-hop poses, pants halfway down their thighs to reveal five different pairs of underwear, bling, muscles, guns. She rendered this in a style derived from fashion ads if they'd been made with the high oil finish of Ingrès, crossed with borrowings from graffiti, fanzines, and the kind of hand-lettered signs you saw in the South, where she'd grown up. Malika both celebrating her subjects and implicating some sort of fixated gaze, Lucien playing with Afro-futurist expectations with an irony you could never put your finger on: it wasn't just me who paid in mental stability for the need to make images in this culture. Some of my old paintings were stored in the racks in Lucien's loft, racks that went all the way to the ceiling. I didn't want to look at them, I knew it wasn't time yet—I knew they were there and I remembered what they looked like but I wasn't sure if the memory was accurate and I was afraid to find out. I don't mean to accuse Lucien or Malika of pandering to the marketplace, I'm just talking about the crazy-making binary of complicity and resistance in selling art at all. Maybe the skeleton with the TV was just for fun. Maybe it was for his daughter's birthday party, or next Halloween.

There was a painting of Lucien's, still unfinished, on the wall across from the windows, the ground a hazy gold applied thinly enough that you could see the canvas through the brushwork. Here and there were little centers of interest—orbs or smudged lozenges in black, dark red, green—ganglia shapes, maybe referencing Miró, only muddied in a way that suggested something like disenchantment tinged with nostalgia. He'd told me about this painting and I could see now that the reason he'd stalled out on it was because one little section was too perfect. It needed to be less correct—he needed to work around or obliterate that little perfect area but he hadn't built up the nerve to kill it yet. All this thinking was making me crave the process of painting, which I didn't want to crave. I saw now that what Lucien's painting needed was the cheap mustard yellow of hot dog stands. I looked at the oil tubes there on his work cart, and decided to mix up what I thought was required, all impulse now, planning to just leave a glob of it there on the palette with a little note, but that isn't what I did. What I did was make a mark on the actual canvas, right in the middle of the little perfect area, bright yellow, as stark as a cigar burn. It was maybe a centimeter in circumference, a quick three stabs from a flat hog hair brush, a little violation in three acts. I meant it as a favor, even if Lucien wouldn't see it that way, at least not for a while, though I thought he would see it that way eventually—eventually he would understand that it was really just my way of saying hi, I was here, see you next time, thank you for everything you've given me.

3

There was a text from Ana on my phone, *Why aren't you picking up?* along with five missed calls (my voice mail was full).

It was about 1:30 in the afternoon when I got back to the Island. I looked through the glass doors at the woods beyond my backyard and remembered walking through that same space when it was barren in early spring and seeing Ana the first time, standing in Jack's driveway as the neighbor's dog began to bark. My kitchen was still, the maple floors gleaming in the August sunlight, and it occurred to me I had developed a habit of standing there: that was how Ana would usually come over, walking through the woods to the sliding glass door at the back of the house, where I would be waiting, unless I was trying to sit calmly in the living room, or on the patio outside. There'd been fireflies the last few weeks, an improbable electric green, and sometimes we'd just sit there at the glass table at night in my uncomfortable outdoor chairs and watch them, some music on, kerosene burning in the camping lanterns with that faintly sulfurous smell. You could see the moon and a smudge of stars on a field of bluish black sky through the branches of the trees. Ana would smoke a joint and sometimes we'd walk down to the dock in the dark and sit with our feet in the water and look at the stars over the pond, where they shone far more brightly. The yard would look unnaturally still when we came back. I had torches, not tiki torches but long stainless-steel posts that ended in expanding spirals that held small glass lamps filled with citronella oil. They would be burning there for the empty yard, the abandoned table and chairs. The obstacles of national borders, visas, the distance between New York and Mexico City—none of that compared to what I'd let out of myself in Lucien's loft, I thought, which seemed repellent and endless, but there was only a little time left for Ana and me, and I knew the only way not to waste more of it was to call her, which I did, standing there in the kitchen. She asked if I was all right and I asked her the same thing. Charlottesville, that had been the main focus of her weekend, she said. I told her I'd had a similar time and that I'd gone to the city for a change of scenery and that I'd just gotten home.

"Sorry," I said. "I just forget about my phone sometimes. As you have noticed, no doubt."

"You could try turning it on."

"No, I think it was on. I don't know, maybe not."

"I have something to tell you."

"What?"

"I don't know if I want to tell it to you. It's embarrassing."

"Embarrassing how?"

"I don't think I can see you for a while. I mean, I feel like I might need to go to a doctor. That was part of the reason I was calling you all those times. I have these—*es una erupción*—my feet, my ankles, I don't know what it is. *Hiedra venenosa.* Like . . . a poison plant?"

"You mean poison ivy?"

"Maybe. Yes. But it's bad."

"How bad?"

"No, it's really bad."

I ended up driving to her in my truck instead of walking through the woods, because I thought I might need to take her to the urgent-care place or at least go to a pharmacy in town. It was actually harder to get to Jack's house by car than by foot—you had to get on the main road, making a left turn into thick summer traffic, then take another immediate left just a few dozen yards later. Jack's street started out paved then became a dirt road with grass growing between the tire ruts. There was a fountain in his front yard, frolicking cupids around a cement bowl, that kind of thing, though I didn't see any water, so maybe it was more of a statue than a fountain. I parked the car and when Ana opened the front door she looked at me through the crack, standing there in the dimness. She had her hair pulled back, though strands of it had come loose and hung about her face. I could tell she hadn't showered. Somehow I would forget what she looked like in various subtle ways and then be surprised by the reality of her. She wore a white tank top made of ribbed cotton and khaki shorts, and as I stood in the doorway she was staring at me in the same way I was staring at her, which made me uncomfortable.

"It's probably not poison ivy," I said, when I stepped to the door. "It's on both your feet?"

She didn't dignify this with a response, but touched the side of my face. She was trying to make me accept what was happening between us, and I was resisting, not wanting to resist, not knowing why I was.

"Jack left early," she said. "I wish I could have gone to the city with you."

"I literally had the least interesting time you could possibly have there."

"What did you do?"

"Picture a TV that's not on. Now picture that for two days."

"Come on."

"Now picture the two days without even the TV."

What she had was not poison ivy but a thick cluster of tiny wounds made by insects—chiggers—so small you couldn't see them. She had dozens of them on her feet and ankles, little translucent bumps. I knew from experience that they would get much worse in the next day or two and might not go away entirely before she left the country.

"They lay eggs that live inside your skin?" she asked, after I explained.

"No, it's not that bad. They just inject you with something that eats away at your skin and that's what they feed on."

"I can't take it."

"They're going to itch. I'm sorry. They're going to be really uncomfortable."

"Haha."

"I know, they're already uncomfortable. There are a few tricks, we'll make the best of it."

We wanted to have sex, in spite of this, so we did. I had never been in Jack's house and now I was with Ana in the living room, on a couch that must have originated with Jack's parents, because everything in that room was old, the couch smothered in a floral-print cover, but what made that room more than just a collection of secondhand furniture and garbage—seashells in bowls, sailing trophies, moldering quilts—was the huge panel of windows on the side facing the pond, covered now by long vertical blinds that had been drawn to make a wall of lustrous black, like ink, swirled with the reflected light of the table lamp whose beaded switch ended in a small wooden whale. Ana's body was starkly lit in the places where that lamplight hit it directly and stark in a different way everywhere else. She was on top of me and I switched off the lamp and the shadows in the ambient light from the hallway defined her angles and curves like a woodcut. She had bangs, I don't know if I made that clear before, and the way her pulled-back hair came loose from its rubber band and was black and tufted together by sweat, made me feel for a moment like we were in some stylized film from fifty years ago. I had to pull myself away from that and look at what was really there, her tits above her rib cage, her collarbone and the bones of her shoulders. She was pounding on my chest and letting out loud high gasps that made me feel like she was fucking somebody who wasn't quite there, but I grabbed her ass in both my hands and she let her fingers trail over my body and I stopped thinking about it, moving in the shadows and the faint yellow glow from the hallway of someone else's house.

She said she'd had a dream about Malika. When I asked her how that was possible, or what Malika had looked like in the dream, she said she didn't know how it was possible but that Malika was very beautiful, though also small, doll-like, and then she admitted that she knew what Malika looked like because she'd gone on the internet. Malika in a turban (I knew they came from Ghana), Malika with her hair down in braids, Malika standing in front of a blinged-out Mustang in

Atlanta. It was when Ana mentioned the picture with the car that I began to feel the tension I felt whenever I tried to imagine Malika approving of my continuing on as I'd continued. Malika's voice had been a little pinched and nasal, higher in pitch than you might expect. To be the smartest person or the only smart person in a high school in a small southern town can make you stiff, camouflaging your vulnerability and oddness with bland or folksy correctness—it's the story of almost every white politician from those places, as well as many who aren't white. Malika had a small bit of that. That was perhaps why she dressed the way she did, flaunting the side of herself that she valued and wanted known, the flamboyant side. Toward the end of her life, there was this spiral in which the more outraged her work grew, the more appealing it became to buyers. Perhaps she was trying to do things with art that can't be done. We used to talk about it, and it would make me uncomfortable with my abstractions, which felt even older and more decrepit than ever, in need of renewal, which is always painful.

"Malika wasn't that small," I said. "She was about your size."

We were back at my house now, Jack's house having become immediately uncomfortable after we'd had sex.

"She was small in the dream. Not surprising, I guess. Small and harmless."

"She actually had kind of a forcefulness. Also like you."

"I don't think I'm that forceful."

"Not as in coercive. I mean forceful as in you noticed her, she drew people's attention."

"It wasn't a dream I wanted to have. Maybe it was just my punishment for looking around in your private life."

"Whatever that is."

"It didn't change anything about how I feel about you."

"What happened in the dream?"

"She tried to kill me."

"Right."

"I'm just kidding. If it was that kind of dream, I wouldn't be telling you about it. We were more like friends, simpatico. We were just swimming in a swimming pool together, maybe at a hotel. Somehow we could whisper things to each other through the water. I read about you, too."

"On the internet."

"You had an argument. It's all right, people argue."

"I'm not sure I want to talk about it right now."

"It's a lot."

"I don't blame myself for what happened. There may be some people who do, but I'm not one of them. Not in a literal way. In other ways, obviously, yes, failing someone you love, not being with them when they die. That is not easy."

It was not even dusk yet, but my living room got poor natural light so it already seemed like evening. I had scoffed at the furnishings in Jack's house, and to a lesser degree I had scoffed at Lucien's loft, but anyone could have scoffed at my own living room, with its clutter of paintings from friends, Malika's souvenirs—folk art made out of mirrors and tin cans, woven baskets, a Dogon mask—and the big red rug with its Zulu patterns, the low leather stools. It was the most peaceful room I'd ever been in, and Ana was lying there on the green couch with her itchy feet, her laptop on the coffee table next to a glass of iced hibiscus tea. I had been watching her watch a video, pretending I was paying attention to the film, Ana's feet in a pair of my socks which I'd persuaded her to put on after slathering her insect bites with clear calamine lotion. The socks kept the air off the bites. It helped minimize the itching. The movie we'd been watching was a documentary about the Living Theatre called *Signals Through the Flames.* It had been a favorite of Malika's, which seemed like an odd coincidence, until Ana told me that it had just appeared in a column of suggested videos on her YouTube page, and I realized that this coincidence was probably in fact a result of surveillance—a result of Ana googling Malika's name.

She died in a car accident on her way down to visit her family and then her brother Jesse at the prison. This was what Ana would have read on the internet, that Malika Jordan's partner, the artist Christopher Bell, had let her drive off by herself in a rainstorm after an argument, as shown in text messages with one of her friends and interviews with some of her other friends, who said that Bell was a moody person, jealous of Malika's growing reputation, and who had let her drive by herself in a rainstorm rather than accompany her on a family visit, even though he knew that Malika didn't like to drive, that it scared her. There is a kind of image that is not quite art but the construction by others of who we are in this world. It would have been mentioned that Christopher Bell was not my birth name, that I had been born in Israel. My physical appearance did not signify what some people thought it might signify but maybe something more like the opposite, though these were people who did not know much about the country in which I was born, where there are Israelis who are culturally Arab or African and Arabic-speakers who are Jews. I wished we could go back to the moment before *Signals Through the Flames* came up on Ana's screen.

Malika was embracing her rage, I went on with Ana, having spent much of her life repressing it. It caused friction between us, because she thought I was judging her (it was impossible to parse out if I judged her or not, if I did it in spite of myself and was just blind to it, in denial). The urge to make images, so simple in itself, is never simple in practice. The exhibition that had made Malika's name before her death was called *Millions of Dead Cops*—it was an experiment with the limits of directness, and for the gallery an experiment with the limits of exploitativeness. There were going to be threats on Malika's and others' lives and the gallery was going to show the work anyway, beneath a flag not of profit but of political protest and free expression. Cops shot by snipers from trees in what could have been Los Angeles but also could have been Baghdad. Cops blown up in their station house or torched alive in the squad car. The paintings recalled Goya in their fierceness and luster, but I worried they would entrap and define Malika forever. When I was her age, I showed a series of paintings about my recovery, and perhaps because I was making paintings that referenced loaded subjects (crack rock versus powder cocaine, for example), I was asked about my childhood, as in my ethnic identity, and I explained that my project was partly about my confusion in that realm. I never met my father, my mother was unstable, I had moved through many different families and places growing up, and I had thoughts about identity that I couldn't articulate in words. You could say that any clarity about my identity was beaten out of me every day at school when I was young because of how I looked and how I spoke, and this taught me that words like *identity* and *American* are somehow very meaningful and very meaningless at the same time. It wasn't that Malika and I had a fight. It was that our last disagreement had gone deep and we hadn't resolved it, and so it existed for me now like a room that got larger and dimmer the more time I spent in it.

"I don't think what happened was an accident," I said.

"What do you mean?"

"I mean I think someone ran her off the road."

"What?"

"It's not an idea, it's a feeling."

"It seems impossible."

"Not to me."

She'd been struggling against the itching, and now she couldn't stand it anymore. She got up off the sofa, half staggering like someone about to be sick, and headed to the bathroom, trailing one hand behind her as if telling me to hold my thought. The only thing that helped was to sit on the edge of the bathtub, take off the socks, and run her feet under the cool water. I went in to check on her after a while and found her like that, her ankle and foot in her hands, her eyes pressed shut, tears coming out at the corners.

4

had told her before about how I never came home at night, even out here, without wondering if I would be confronted by the police for breaking into my own house. I had told her that I once had a close friend, an older artist who had important information I wanted but whose studio had no buzzer, you had to yell up to him through the window so that he could throw the keys down, and I found myself not going there after a while, the ordeal of waiting not worth it, the feeling of my own conspicuousness. After 9/11, people sometimes spoke to me as if I were slightly mentally unstable because they couldn't place me and because I looked a little like Osama bin Laden, I just did and still do. In my rational mind, I didn't believe Malika had actually been murdered, but I also didn't see it as an accident. It was not unlike the young woman killed by the car in Charlottesville. I didn't see anything random in either of those deaths.

I went down to the pond. The sun was setting and the water and the trees behind it were two hazy fields of color, one a salmon orange, the other a muddy green, both eerily still beneath a third field which was the oyster-hued sky, all of it uncanny in a way that reminded me of a Polaroid left in someone's drawer. The clouds were always distinctive there, with the low canopy of the Island's East End, and now a bright white wispy formation loomed above me like a portal, or a tiara, or a mouth. I hadn't gone to the hospital after Malika's car crash because it was too late, but I still had a memory of her cereal bowl sitting in our kitchen sink, bearing traces of the instant porridge she liked to eat, Malt-O-Meal, which I couldn't deal with until much later, after I came back from her funeral. Back in the bathroom, running her feet under the bathtub faucet, Ana had apologized for bringing up Malika. Everything between us had started out so lighthearted, carefree, that it was odd to look back on it three months later and also find it careless. I lived closer to the bay than to the ocean, and I remember that one night after we drove there we took off our shoes and walked along the edge of the water, which lit up blue here and there with the glow of phosphorescent jellyfish. There was a kind of sand cliff you hiked down to get to the beach and someone had managed to drive a car down it, a

Porsche, which had been abandoned near the surf seemingly undamaged. They had gotten it down there but couldn't get it back up. It sat in the dark like some strange monument of a vanished world.

She had turned on all the lights in the living room and the kitchen, when I came back in the house, filling the place with a yellow blaze. There was music playing on the stereo, a band from Venezuela that made a kind of camp disco rock I never understood but that I knew worked for Ana as a remedy against homesickness. I guess the simplest thing to say about that music is that it was the sound of joy. If you found joy embarrassing—and there were times when I found even the word embarrassing—then you would not like the music or the sight of Ana dancing to it, but there was a kind of relief for me now in not hating it—the rolling bass, the big operatic orgasm of sound. She pointed at the ceiling with one hand while pointing at the floor with the other, pausing melodramatically in her dance, not looking at me, letting me deal with it.

"I can't decide if I should smoke or not," she said. "I want to get high but I don't know if it will just make me focus on the itching more."

The name of the song was "La Vecina," I remembered then, "The Neighbor," about a man who falls in love with a beautiful woman who lives across the way.

"I'm not going to ask you to come to Mexico," she said, "but have you ever thought about that?"

"I'd like to come."

"That's not what I asked."

"I'd like to visit you."

"Is that what this is to you, a visit?"

I didn't know how we'd got here so I didn't answer.

"Everyone is so surprised when I tell them I'm going back to Mexico. They can't understand why. They think of poor people dying in the desert, trying to get across the border. Narcos. That's the only idea they have."

I could tell somehow that we were both thinking of a time when I'd misremembered the president of Venezuela's name, mispronounced it, and Ana had told me that that was how it had been for her here, people's eyes glazing over not with boredom but with simple absence, the inability to hear even the simplest information about a place they didn't want to know more about. More than three million people had fled Venezuela, she'd said. People asked why she would want to go back to Mexico rather than trying everything possible to stay here, as if their puzzlement itself didn't answer their question. In Mexico, she said, there were terrible problems, but at least she didn't have to hate people for their innocence.

She said she was hungry, so I went into the kitchen to make her something to eat. She stood there in a pair of my socks, not watching me but closing her eyes and listening to the music. She'd told me once about a Sunday television show in Venezuela, which sometimes went on for four or five hours, in which the nation's leader, dressed in a red button-down shirt, would hold forth on whatever came to mind, or just publicly berate his subordinates, who sat before him in similar red shirts. Planes hit the towers. The Nazis entered Paris. The price of oil fell and Caracas burned. I fried some eggs after scrambling them in a bowl with milk. They were Jerome's eggs, the rich yellow spreading for Ana in the pan.

5

She stayed at my house after that, that place full of Malika's art and souvenirs and furniture and even clothes in storage. Ana's toothbrush looked strange to me beside mine on the sink, her cosmetics bag with its bottles and tubes visible through the clear plastic—these objects seemed to short-circuit time, though in fact they extended it, revealed the extent of my dormancy. Ana ended up sleeping downstairs on the couch most nights because of her bites, which kept her up at all hours, and after a couple of attempts to sleep in the chair beside her it began to seem ridiculous not to just sleep in my bed, where, alone, I again confronted the sense of my house as an unconscious reliquary. One night during all this, just before I went upstairs, we heard the sounds of Sebastian and my neighbor Diana arguing, her shouting loud enough that we could hear it through the storm door, causing us to stand there for a while looking through the wire mesh and glass panes out into black darkness. To go outside seemed to cross over into an invasion of privacy, and in any case the shouting eventually stopped, there was silence, but then from the living room we saw car headlights, a white smudge through the black glaze of the windows—it was either his car or hers, those were the only possibilities. We didn't see either of them the next morning. After a day or two, I guessed Sebastian was gone because his car was never in the driveway and he and Diana never came out on the front lawn, where they always liked to spend time together, though his ragged end table and his stereo console remained sitting in the grass, still unrestored, still junk, just debris as before.

"You've only been here for a little while," I said to Ana one night as she lowered her feet into the water.

"A lot has happened."

"You don't like it here, you kind of hate it. I get that."

"I don't like hating people. It's a strong word."

"You shouldn't scratch so much. How do you say *chigger* in Spanish?"

"*Mamahuevo.*"

"*Mamahuevo*? What about *hate*?"

"*Odio.*"

A letter had arrived from the governor of Jesse's state saying that his pardon request had received a hearing scheduled for November 18 at 8:00 a.m. I hadn't told Ana about Jesse, nor had I told Jesse about Ana. To bring it up now would just be to invoke Malika again, but that didn't explain or excuse my previous silence, which cast suspicion over my silence now.

We lay in bed that night entwined with each other in the sheets. Sometimes when we had sex, I would find myself gripping the ball of Ana's heel, not wanting to leave out even that part of her.

"What was your name?" she asked. "Your birth name."

I told her and at first she thought I was joking.

"My mother is not right," I said.

"Why did she want to move here?"

"She wanted to be famous. There was fame where we were, but not New York City fame. She didn't really think it through. And she wouldn't have used that word. *Fame.* Typical provincial mistake. We left Israel when I was ten and after that I grew up in New York and I spoke bad English and I had this dark skin because it turns out my father was actually from Tunisia. I never met him. No one knew what I was, it took me a long time to find my way, trying to have friends and then get laid and all that. Those kids really wanted to kill me. I had to learn to deal with it, and that meant sort of jumping into the fear, risking your body in order to survive."

"When was the last time you saw your mother?"

"A long time ago."

"Years?"

"A long time. Maybe ten years. I hardly ever think about her."

The day before Ana left I went down to check the mail again, and when I came back up the street I saw her at the edge of the footpath that went down to the pond. She'd found a box turtle lying upside down in the leaves and didn't know what to do—it wasn't moving, and even when we tramped closer, it still didn't move. We stared for a while at the intricate pattern of black and orange on the bottom of its shell, its feet etched with tiny black scales. I took a stick and poked the leaves next to it and it still didn't move—it didn't move because it wasn't a turtle. It was just a facsimile of a turtle, a very realistic-looking plastic toy for a child.

"It would have made sense to you if I stayed," she said. "But the other way around, you leaving here, that never even occurred to you."

There were tears in her eyes, but mostly she was angry, even though just a moment before we'd been laughing. I tried to hold her and she went still, or that's what I thought as I stood there looking at the plastic turtle. But then she hit me in the chest and turned away, and I saw I had missed something crucial about myself all this time, and that it was too late now to change it.

I drove Ana to the airport the next day.

6

By the end of September, the weeds on the pond floor had grown tall enough that they slithered against you when you swam, though I wasn't swimming much after Ana left, I was hardly going out at all. The college I taught at was near the Shinnecock reservation, on the other side of the highway. My class met there for three hours once a week in the late afternoon, a group of six young painters, most of whom came out here all the way from the city. The fiercest and best critics were never very good artists, and the best artists were the worst critics because whatever they had at that point was not theorized, just intuitive. They must have thought I was stoned most of the time, though I tried, despite my certainty that none of it mattered. Jesse had wanted to be a teacher, it had been more than twenty years ago. I saw that part of what tied me to this place, whether it made sense or not, was my connection to Jesse and through Jesse to Malika—I knew if I ever left that things between Jesse and me would somehow slip, I would fall into a different kind of life and make less contact, and he would still be where he was and I would be farther away.

About three weeks after Ana left, there was a terrible earthquake in Mexico that destroyed dozens of buildings and left many people dead, including in Ana's neighborhood, as I learned in an email she sent me. Until then, she had not responded to my emails or phone calls but after the earthquake she finally wrote a brief message to say she was all right and to thank me for checking. There was this formality, then more silence. Whatever I felt that fall after she left was like an illness, though it was an illness I wanted to prolong because it was the only feeling I could imagine ever having. I would walk around with her name flashing like a marquee in my mind. It kept me up at night, but it also felt like my life had finally been stripped down and purified to just the hard dry essence.

Jesse's hearing was that November, a few days before Thanksgiving. To get to the airport, I took the highway for sixty miles without highlights until I finally saw the stretch of restaurants with names like Saipan or Ali Baba on lighted signs. The three-hour flight landed in a place too hot for the plane's climate control, and when I disembarked the sound of jazz came though the speakers on my way past the food court to baggage claim. I drove a rental car to a hotel, then very early the next morning I drove out of the city past petroleum storage tanks and synthetics plants with furnaces that shot bright flames into the sky, through cypress swamps—ash-colored trees and blue-black water—then on and on past gas stations that sold chicken parts, boiled peanuts, thick pine forests with the occasional church made of wooden boards, raised up on pilings for when the river flooded. Jesse's time in prison had now been twenty-two years, and the journey I'd made from my house seemed like a kind of visualization of how long that was. I thought of a passage from Malika's artist's book, *Darkadia*, text surmounting and intruding on a drawing of the open mouth of a whale: *There is no outside, there is no crowd, even you are only real to yourself.*

I parked in the lot of the courts complex about an hour south from where Jesse was—his and Malika's family were at the prison, where they could stand in the same room as Jesse to show their support, while the pardon board convened where I was, in the state capital—the process happened by a kind of live telecast between the two locations. I signed in with a state policeman in a blue uniform who told me to go back to my car and leave my wallet and phone and everything else but my car keys and license locked in the glove box. When I came back, a sheriff's deputy gave me a green placard to show I had come in support of an "offender"—the green indicated that I wanted them to let Jesse "go"—while others who had come for different reasons received red placards that meant "stop." We waited all together in a large hot room without phones or books or magazines. As the day wore on, the room got still hotter and two incarcerated men in jumpsuits on work release came in and set up two large drum fans to cool the air. The roar was so loud I couldn't hear the tumult that had just erupted on the other side of the wall in the room where a hearing was taking place. Some city police arrived. It turned out that a family member of a man whose request for parole had just been denied had thrown a chair at the DA, then stormed off and punched a spider web into the glass door leading back out into the courtyard. I heard this from Jesse's lawyer. He had a large file folder bulging with documents, and while we waited he kept getting bored in his perusal of them and sometimes spoke to me, curious that I'd come from New York, where he'd once spent a vacation. I went to the commissary at the end of the hall and bought myself a cold drink. I hadn't picked the lawyer but I was paying part of his fees. Hours went by in that waiting room. There was no way to tell when I would be called because no one knew. Eventually, late that afternoon, I was admitted into the chambers and took a seat in a row of chairs along with the lawyer. The members of the pardon board, all men, sat at a long desk to my left, facing the video monitor where Jesse was onscreen. He wore a pale blue prison work shirt with long sleeves, buttoned all the way to the throat but with no tie, something ritualistic about his posture that suggested shackles, though I knew he wasn't in shackles. He sat at a table with his hands in his lap between a white guard and a white warden with no expressions on their faces. I thought of times many years before when I'd woken up in rooms with some stranger breathing next to me through an open mouth, or with no one with me at all, just the unfamiliar furniture, my dry lips stuck to my teeth, my fingertips burned. I knew that getting high, aware of the consequences, could feel like a rare form of magnificence. I knew it was the drugs the board would fixate on: Jesse and some other young men gathered on the porch after dark on the night of the crime, getting high.

One of the men on the raised platform asked Jesse about substance abuse and anger management classes. Another asked him about the letter of apology he'd written to his victim, who was not opposing Jesse's clemency, but now the man pressed harder anyway. He asked Jesse about the night he and his friend had showed up at the young woman's house at three o'clock in the morning to rob her at gunpoint. Jesse kept silent for such a long time that I wondered if he'd heard.

I must have been nervous and that's why I can't remember the hearing itself as clearly as I remember the time in the waiting room. What should be the most vivid part of the day comes back to me in melodramatic stills, like those renderings made by courtroom sketch artists. What I saw between

Jesse and the men on the raised platform seemed to go beyond antagonism or even cynicism to become a kind of intimacy. They were there to perform, and in order to perform they had to feel at least some amount of real abasement and real condemnation, even if they understood the feelings were just part of a game. The state had spent half a million dollars to keep Jesse locked up for a crime in which no one was hurt, a three-hundred-dollar robbery, and if they were to justify not spending maybe a million more, these were the necessary rituals. *I took the substance abuse class. I took the anger management class.* What he couldn't say was that the only fact of anything close to real significance was that he wasn't nineteen anymore.

They commuted his life sentence to ninety-nine years. It seemed like a distinction without a difference, but it meant he could apply for parole after he'd served twenty-five. Three more years of waiting, in other words. My confusion must have shown because later a man on the board turned and spoke to me, explaining that this was good news.

The Jordans, Malika's family, lived about two and a half hours from the courts building, in the opposite direction from that of the airport I would use to get back home. I stopped first at my hotel, a long, low-slung building with brick pillars and steel fire doors that looked similar to the buildings I had just left. A dim fluorescent light fixture shone on me while I washed my face. I remembered the last time I'd visited Jesse there were logistical problems getting him from his camp to the shed and our time was shortened. When they summoned everyone to leave later that afternoon, I made a stupid joke as Jesse and I stood at the exit, his door to the right, where he would be strip-searched, and mine to the left, where I would stand in a locked sally port waiting for a white bus to take me away. There was some spatial confusion as we moved to our respective sides, and the joke I made was asking Jesse if he wanted to trade places. He didn't laugh, and when I went to hug him, he was extending his hand to shake, and we awkwardly did some combination of both, so that I walked away feeling as if the whole visit had not quite really happened or had been mostly erased. I sat on the bed and pressed my hands to my eyes until I thought I heard something moving back in the bathroom. When I looked, I saw Ana standing in the doorway in Malika's clothes, a few braids falling over her sutured face, her eyes unseeing glass. She was there for a moment the way a dream is there. *If you are wise, you are wise for yourself. If you scoff, you alone will bear it.* Jesse had sent this to me in an email, a line from Proverbs. I didn't know what he meant by it, I knew only that right now I didn't feel I belonged with his family, and that this feeling was familiar, but I also knew I had to go see them. I never deserved Malika, but after a while you have to accept things as they are.

Her mother's house was a shotgun raised up on cinder

blocks with a nearly destroyed Nissan, probably Malika's brother Stephon's, parked on one side. The living room was so dark and the floor so cluttered with objects that I had to concentrate as I stepped inside. I had spoken briefly on the phone with Malika's sister, Sherril, after the hearing, but I had somehow beaten her and her daughters here (they had stopped for food, I learned later), and Stephon and his girlfriend were sitting on the couch watching TV, smoking cigarettes and getting high. He asked if I wanted anything to drink and I said no, then I asked where his mother was and he said she was in her bedroom, it had been a long day. All she heard was the three more years, he said. I told him it was hard to figure out how to feel.

"I know how I feel," he said. "I feel like we motherfucking won. Some serious light-at-the-end-of-the-tunnel shit. That's how I feel."

He was high and, along with the smoke in the air, this realization made me want to get high myself or at least have a cigarette. Stephon had a shaven head that showed the scars from a brain surgery he'd had as a child. His girlfriend said she had to go, and so eventually it was just me and him sitting in front of the TV, Stephon idly moving from channel to channel, still smoking. He had a way of making unexpected or disconnected statements in a tone of rigid common sense, looking at me through thick glasses like a high school science teacher.

"Charles Manson," he said. "You heard? They can't stop talking about him now."

"I guess I heard he died."

"He died yesterday. These people keep saying how mysterious he was. 'Inscrutable.' The motherfucker was trying to set off a race war. All those white kids going in people's houses with knives, there's nothing mysterious about that."

"'Inscrutable.'"

"You want some of this?"

"What?"

"You still don't smoke, huh?"

"No."

"No buffer."

"I've been that way a long time."

"I guess, what, you develop a tolerance for boredom. Like a really high tolerance."

"It's kind of like fasting for a long time. Then it's like fasting for a long time while you're holding your breath."

I hadn't seen Stephon since Malika's funeral and he hardly registered then, he was just more dissonance in a time of trauma, and so part of the friction I felt now might have been payback for my indifference then, but another part was who he was and who I was. The story had always been that Stephon had fallen apart when Jesse went to prison, that he stayed in his room for a few years and never quite went back to normal.

"Jonathan Jackson," he said. "You know that story? The

baby brother of George Jackson, the Soledad Brother. How one day he stormed the courthouse with a duffel bag full of weapons, took the judge and a few other hostages, demanded George's release from prison. The people shot him and his partners in the getaway van—killed them all, killed the judge they took hostage. I don't know how I live with myself sometimes when I think of Jonathan Jackson."

"They killed him. They killed George, too."

"That's not what I'm talking about."

"My point is I'm glad you and Jesse are alive."

"Again, not what I'm talking about."

He wanted to show me something, he said, and we went into the garage, which was even more cluttered and chaotic than the living room, though it was better lit, gray light leaking in through two thin windows. I had known places like it since childhood—whatever family, belonging to whomever my mother happened to be fucking at the time, in whose house I was an appendage. Stephon sifted through a stack of boxes, wedged in by tool chests and black garbage bags full of shoes and clothes, a shop vac, a bass guitar with three strings on it that he said he was trying to learn how to play. He found a tablet computer with a smashed screen, smudged with dust, saying he'd been looking for it, did I think he could get it fixed? I was thinking I would wait for Sherril and her daughters to arrive, then stay for a few more minutes, then find a graceful way to leave, but they still weren't there, and then they still weren't there, and I became fixated on my desire for one of Stephon's cigarettes, until eventually my whole perception centered around that one tiny point.

"What time is it?" he said.

"I don't know, eight?"

"You coming back?"

"What do you mean?"

"I was just trying to find a photo album, some pictures of Jesse and me as kids, but it must have got lost. I guess, what, tomorrow. We'll see what that's like. I don't really know."

We stood there a little longer, neither of us knowing what to say, until without looking at me Stephon turned and headed out of the garage. Leaving was always an option for me, leaving whenever I wanted, that was the confrontation he avoided putting into words.

7

As I pulled off the main road onto my little street, after driving back from the airport, I saw my neighbor Diana's daughter standing on the corner in the cold, hands stuffed into the pockets of a football jacket, her breath visible as steam against the overcast sky. The whole subdivision had once been part of a boys' camp that dated back to World War II, a place for kids with polio, nothing but a few cabins in the woods, all of that gone now. I didn't recognize Diana's daughter, she just looked like someone waiting for the county bus or maybe hitchhiking, but she was still there later when I walked down to get my mail, and she said hello and even seemed to remember me fondly, as though we had an interesting shared past, of which I had no memory at all. Randomness—that conveyed better than any other word the patchwork quality of my street, which was not a "neighborhood." I remember finding clumps of asphalt in the soil when I went to dig up some dead bushes and later I learned from Jerome that one of the previous owners used to run a taxi business there and had paved over all the lawns for his cars. That evening, as I was sitting in my living room looking out at piles of dead leaves I had raked a week ago but not yet taken to the dump, I saw the lights of a police car as it passed my house then continued on to the one Diana rented in. The blue slashed across the cypress trees between my house and the road, off then on, off then on. When I heard what happened later from Jerome and then from Diana, I remembered seeing Diana's daughter standing out there in the cold in her football jacket and feeling no sense of urgency and I wondered what that said about me. Leslie was her daughter's name, Diana reminded me that night after the police left—it rhymed with Nestlé, she said. Before this, Diana had been working outside all that day putting down compost on other people's gardens, moving it in wheelbarrows from the back of a dump truck, then spreading it with a spade and a rake, the temperature in the forties, the sun starting to set at four. Her daughter had run off with her boyfriend, Darren, she told me. We were talking through my storm door, Diana standing there in the stark light of the single bulb, fear charging the air around her, her face wet, and I was still deciding whether or not to ask her to come in when my phone rang. I used to make paintings about these congestions of synchronicity, discordant collisions of events that revealed a deeper disorder. It was Jesse on the phone. I let Diana into the house because I was preoccupied with answering, out of some default politeness, and we stood there in my living room now with its red Zulu carpet, Malika's paintings and collected objects on the walls, as I pressed "1" to accept the call—it didn't work and I pressed it again. I gestured to Diana to sit down on the green couch where Ana used to lie watching videos on her laptop, a pair of my socks on her feet, and I thought of a box of Ana's mandarin orange tea that was still in my cupboard, I could see the black-and-gold packaging in my mind. Jesse's voice always sounded flat and unreadable at the beginning of our conversations. We hadn't spoken since his hearing and now we made small talk as I brought Diana a glass of water. Three months of rehab, all for nothing, Diana told me later, about her daughter, Leslie. The two of them were really trying this time, she said— she thought they were making it work, she didn't force Leslie to get a job right away, told her she could just sit around for a while, take it easy. Leslie and Darren were going up the Island to buy drugs, she said. Fentanyl. Heroin. They were in a red Honda Fit that she described in more detail so I could "keep an eye out for it." Jesse was telling me about a friend of his now, Travis, whom I'd met, a small man with a shaven head whose face reminded me a little of a tortoise because of its prominent nose and close-set eyes, Travis who ran a scam out of the visiting shed, stealing hamburgers and chicken patties and other food to sell to inmates who would cook it themselves and sell it for less than they charged in the shed. He told me now that Travis was dead. He got caught with some of the stolen food and was sent to lockdown, where he and his cellmate got high and everything went crazy. What they smoked was called "mojo," he said, a form of synthetic marijuana, like bath salts, and after they smoked it Travis's cellmate bashed Travis's head open right on the concrete floor—they were not even enemies, Jesse told me, they were more like friends—but now Travis was dead because of some minor write-up over chicken patties. The car was stolen, the red Honda, Diana told me later, and eventually I learned that Leslie's boyfriend, Darren, crashed it the next morning after they spent the night at a shared house just a couple miles west of us. They started walking through the woods, the boyfriend's nose broken, until they found the trail put in by the county a few years ago and then they tried to make it to Diana's house, winding their way through the deep thicket where white pines lay dead beneath the oaks, their limbs bleached like bones, vines climbing toward the telephone wires—old cans, the black husks of burned-out coals, a faded scrap of T-shirt listing at the edge of someone's yard. The boyfriend broke into an empty house and stole some clothes because they were freezing by then. He could see himself in the glass as he approached, dark and slouch-shouldered, then disappearing into his own reflection, a smudge or a shadow pushing open the sliding glass door, feeling entitled to whatever he found, as if he were avenging some basic wrong implicit in those sedate houses whose owners did not even bother to lock their doors. I knew all this about him just from seeing his face on the internet after he and Leslie got arrested. In the city, there is the motion of a million people putting on faces and clothes, doing things very fast, so fast that time implodes, you feel it can never really end, that it can't hurt you, but sometimes on a late November evening, looking out at piles of dead leaves you had raked but not yet taken to the dump, the sky would turn from the color of ash to dense black, as dark as if you'd closed your eyes, and the feeling then was that time had already ended, that you'd been sitting in the quiet room in the armchair for much longer than you realized. I remember waking up on my couch the next morning with my clothes still on, cold and damp, and when I stood up I saw the sliding glass door in the kitchen that Ana used to come through—Ana, whom I had seen that day last spring across the woods in her black parka, as the neighbor's dog, Chloe, started barking and Ana clapped her hands. The sun had risen and the sky outside was the color of milk, the bare trees glowing pink and orange at their edges, and I found myself walking out into it, for I had slept with even my boots on. Someone had stolen Sebastian's old table, Leslie had told me the day before when she was waiting on the side of the road, they'd broken the glass top into a million pieces trying to move it and just left the shards there on the patio. Maybe I should bring my lawn furniture inside or lock it up or something, she'd told me. *I mean, google yourself sometime. Why you live on this shitty street, I'll never understand.* I had walked through the woods now and followed the little road that led to Jack's driveway—the moss between the tire ruts, the disused fountain with its plaster cupids—and I was standing in front of his house, staring into the windows of the empty rooms, wanting to scream and claw at the door, as if Ana were still inside, as if the only problem now was getting her to let me back in.

8

I met a woman on the plane who told me how she'd been thinking, all through the months preceding the last election, about where to go if what she feared would happen did happen. We were in a taxi now from the airport in Mexico City, and I was listening to her but I was also watching through the glass the crude rectangular buildings painted in pastel hues or just bare concrete with a black square or two of paneless windows, plastic tarps covering damaged roofs, billboards made of sheets of vinyl printed with logos and phone numbers. Something about the woman's face when she concentrated reminded me of Malika's sister, Sherril. Leaving would only get harder as her son, who was twelve now, got older, she said, but already she couldn't afford her neighborhood in Brooklyn, where she'd grown up—it was like the sea was rising, there was nowhere left, and if she was going to get out she might as well "really leave-leave, put it behind me." She worked in the modern dance world and had spent a fair amount of time in Cuba, she said, but it was difficult to live there, even if you had money coming from the States, and because she spoke good Spanish she was thinking about Mexico now. I remembered her, an African American woman looking for refuge for herself and her son in Mexico, after I got out of the cab, and that same night I saw her from a distance at a performance by the Ballet Folklórico at the Palacio de Bellas Artes. The theater was full, though not with tourists, it seemed, or at least not with foreigners, but mostly with Mexican families whom I watched as silhouettes as they took their seats in the faint glow of the dimmed lights, the tiered balconies to either side of us interspersed with different-colored marble walls, like an opera house carved out of a mine. Flocks of dancers took the stage in traditional costumes and the orchestra played. I had spent some time that afternoon walking around the city's historic center, the baroque buildings like a dingier Spain on a grander scale. Old-fashioned organ grinders played out-of-tune music in their khaki uniforms and from everywhere came images—tacos de canasta, lollipops, peanut brittle, a ten-peso note with Emiliano Zapata's eyes Xed out in white. When I saw the woman from the taxi now, in a balcony seat far off to my right, her expression struck me as a reflection of my own: we had both chosen this show, somehow patriotic without being disgusting, as a way to avoid the empty silence of our hotel rooms. There were men in charro pants and sombreros, women in flowing dresses whose skirts whirled like capes around their bodies and above their heads. That afternoon, I'd seen insects in a grocer's window, a mural of a dead nun's head wreathed in roses, and before me now, in this theater that had been built for a dictator, a troupe of men in flat-brimmed hats danced in ritual movements, some in ancient masks, carrying gourds, arrows, bows, and I couldn't hold any of it in my mind at the same time as my memory of Ana.

That night I had a dream that I was being led through the woods behind my house by soldiers who'd rounded up others like me, marching us through a clearing where a house appeared with its clapboard siding splintered in places, the gray paint slashed with brown, a broken bicycle cast off into the bushes. One of the prisoners, a young woman, turned and looked at me over her shoulder, smiling so bitterly that she had to cover her face with the corner of her shawl so that I could see only her mocking, glassy eyes. There were more soldiers on the lawn, rifles slung over their backs or leaned up against the trees, looking straight ahead or at the ground and not at the naked girl chained by her wrists and ankles to a metal cot that had been dragged there. We descended into the house's opened cellar doors, where a rectangle of light shone weakly on the far wall, cast there by a slide projector, the projected image the face of the young woman with the sarcastic eyes. I woke up to find myself in a hotel room two stories above the Zócalo in Mexico City.

I took another cab the next morning to the café Ana had chosen for our meeting. It had been eight months since she left New York—she hadn't wanted me to come but I had come anyway, and finally, before I arrived, she agreed to see me. The café was in a quiet neighborhood whose streets were lined with orange trees, ficus trees, bougainvillea. Something about the pale blue sky, the small apartment buildings with their little balconies, some art deco, some older, triggered a feeling of memory that was probably more like déjà vu. I realized that the neighborhood reminded me of certain parts of Tel Aviv, though my memories of Tel Aviv were hazy at best—I didn't think I had any at all until I got to the café. It had dark wooden beams at the entrance, faintly Japanese, and a large outdoor courtyard where young people and fashionably dressed older people sat looking a certain way that had to do with technology, their laptops and phones conveying a kind of breezy omnipotence. I ordered a club soda. A group of kids had a golden retriever that the owner, a high-school-age boy, ignored while some of his girlfriends doted on it, setting out water in a ceramic bowl. I didn't speak Spanish, but I could understand most of what they said just by watching.

I don't know how I expected Ana to look, solemn maybe,

dressed in gray, and though I wasn't quite wrong I was surprised by how my memory of her was once again suddenly revealed to be inaccurate. Her eyes were covered by black sunglasses and she had cut her hair in a different way, one side closely clipped, almost shaved, and the other slanting down toward her shoulders, cyberpunky. She wore jeans and a black-and-white striped T-shirt under an unbuttoned black blouse, boots that came up to her knees. I thought the idea was that we would kiss each other on the cheek, but it ended up turning into something else, and then it became uncomfortable. I told her it was good to see her.

"I used to come here on the weekends," she said, after we sat down. "It's a good place to hang out and read. Quiet."

"It's kind of invisible from the street. I couldn't find it at first."

"There's an art gallery over there. A big one. The biggest one, actually."

"Sort of like the Gagosian. Of here."

"I guess. We can go look at it later if you want."

"I haven't been to one of those places in a long time. I'm not sure they'd let me in."

She looked down at the table between us, the surface a mosaic of small stones in different shades of beige.

"I was joking," I said. "We can go. It might be nice."

"I know you were joking."

"I was just sitting here thinking how this neighborhood

reminded me of Israel for some reason. But now I think that it's just disorienting to be here. Not in a bad way. Just . . ."

"Weird. Obviously. This neighborhood always reminded me of Miami. I've never been to Israel. Wouldn't want to go— one of the few places I would say that about. Is it like what you expected here?"

She had taken off her sunglasses now and was not squinting but almost, so that her eyes had an unintended plaintiveness, a little bit of eyeliner at the corners, her lipstick an expensive clay color that seemed a natural emanation of her skin. I had known people like her my whole adult life, cosmopolitan people from all over the world, but last spring, because we'd met across the woods behind my house, our meeting had seemed improbable and therefore significant. This sense of significance was like identity, something not really true but that became true with time. Now she was dressed exactly like someone for whom none of this mattered very much anymore. It made it hard to think what I was thinking, all this about the woods last spring, the significance.

"I used to live pretty close by to here," she said. "Maybe two kilometers over that way. A nice neighborhood. But I've been living with my mother for the past few months. It's been a strange year."

"I know."

"I made this discovery when I came back here. Speaking of strange. You know the day Malika died was also the last day I was ever in Venezuela. There were protests—I had gone back to be part of that, that's how naïve I still was. I was lucky I didn't get killed. That's how I got these little scars on my arm. These little white zigzags. You must have noticed them."

"We talked about them. I didn't want to ask too many more questions about it. I could tell they made you self-conscious."

She changed the subject, at least I thought so at first, telling me that when she came back to Mexico last summer, the earthquake struck just as she had set up her new apartment. She somehow made it down the stairs—she remembered being terrified that the fire door wouldn't open on the ground floor, it was a joke people made later, how they'd had the same thought, though Ana couldn't remember other people being in the stairwell with her. Her experience was nothing of course compared to being trapped under rubble, or stranded on a high floor with no way down, or simply dead, obliterated— but mixed in with this devastation and terror in her memory, she said, were other memories—of volunteers gathering in the nearby park with hard hats and flashlights, the restaurants setting up as soup kitchens on the sidewalks outside their doors. This solidarity renewed her feeling that this was her true home, doomed or not (any scientist would tell you it was doomed). Later, it turned out her building had severe cracks in the walls and was too dangerous to inhabit anymore. It was dangerous to even go back in to get her things, all of which she had just unpacked a week or so before. That was how she'd ended up living with her mother on the other side of the city. Her mother had been acting odd for several months before this, detached or unemotional, and Ana and her brother, Hernan, thought it was just some sort of depression, but after the earthquake it got more extreme and they learned it was actually a form of early-onset dementia, frontotemporal dementia. She couldn't be left alone because she might hurt herself. One night she put some books and magazines in a heated oven and almost burned the house down. There was no cure or even treatment and her mother was still young, in good health otherwise, likely to live many more years as her mind kept fading away. As she said, it had been a strange year—her building destroyed, her mother ill, and I had not been there, doing whatever I was doing.

My arm still throbbed from where she had squeezed it in our embrace when she first got here. She was looking at nothing, not even the golden retriever, or the green tea she had ordered but still hadn't touched.

"I think you told me the scars happened to you when you were a child," I said.

She put her fingertips on the stems of her sunglasses, which lay there on the table.

"I was dragged behind a dumpster by two men," she said. "*Colectivos.* They start a riot, but they do it in a way that makes it look like the protesters started it. They're connected to the government, like death squads. They could have killed me,

I come from money, they would have wanted to, but maybe that's why they didn't do it, because another woman, a model, an actress, very famous, had just been murdered by ordinary thieves and I think that's maybe why they stopped. They didn't want to share the dishonor of what happened to *la estrella. La deshonra*."

I was trying to establish how much responsibility I had for not knowing this story before, but then I told myself that the whole point of Ana's time in New York had been to try to move past what she was telling me now and reinvent herself as the kind of person she'd been before it happened.

"I went silent on you because I couldn't take any more bullshit," she said. "Is that why you came here? To bring some more bullshit to my life?"

"I guess that's one way of looking at it. Maybe not the most accurate way."

"What is it that you want?"

"'Want.' My experience is that you don't get to choose that. You can just avoid it or not avoid it. Obviously. *Want*. An interesting word."

We tried to go to the art gallery later, but it didn't open, though they told us it was about to, and so we waited, watching a crew of men moving crated works of art into the side entrance, these precious objects encased in black steel and shrink-wrap, placed on wooden pallets and loaded onto a forklift. The absurdity of all that protection and care reminded me of my past, which seemed so distant it was as though I had died. I don't know if I'll be able to describe the rest of that afternoon or if it will just disintegrate in words. When I said that Ana was trying to reinvent herself as the person she'd been earlier, I meant that her essence really was light, almost the opposite of mine, and that was why after we finally left the gallery and started walking and she offered me her vape pen, I said yes instead of no, because I knew that's what she really wanted from me and I also needed to be less like myself. The last time I smoked weed there was no such thing as a vape pen. The only way I had kept sober all these years was through reflexive abstinence, no exceptions, not even weed or a sip of wine, and I felt real fear when I put the plastic tip of the pen to my lips. I expected chaos, a breaking up of signals that would be too much like vertigo. I expected to immediately want more despite this, and I prepared to fight that feeling though I also feared that this would only make the craving worse.

The entrance to Chapultepec Park, where we ended up going on that sunny day by taxi, was brightly colored, like bossa nova music, with stall after stall of candy sellers and men holding huge clusters of mylar balloons in the shapes of hearts, butterflies, superheroes, jewels. Everything gleamed like a cartoon, the trees a blur of yellow and lime, or when you panned your vision out, of olive drab and gold. I realized then that I was just high—high without any angst or even an urge to reflect on it. We were walking past the men with balloons and people selling ice cream, the sun spilling on our faces, and eventually we came across a monument, a half circle of six marble columns like huge spears tipped with blackened bronze, or like surrealist birthday candles around a stone cake, a commemoration of something as ambiguous in that moment as the figures on an ancient urn. I was smiling. The act of smiling made me want to smile more. When I took Ana's hand, she hardly noticed but took mine, and I could tell she felt the same way I did: it was a beautiful day, nothing else mattered.

9

We woke up in the middle of the night, the light too dim for me to even see her features clearly, strands of hair covering her face, so that I wondered how she was breathing so peacefully. Our bodies were still indistinct, still partly asleep, and it was as if we were both looking at ourselves in a dark mirror or mistaking each other for ourselves. We'd been talking a few hours before about how it had felt to give up drugs and this feeling now reminded me of what I'd been trying to describe then, how after a while it wasn't the high I craved but the memory of the high, a sadness more than a craving, a song you can't stop playing. Later, she put her hands over my eyes: the darkness of Caracas in a blackout, sirens in the distance, fires, and I could picture the reflected glare in the streets below—white, then red, then black—the fear objectified in the building's silence.

Her hair was greasy on my fingertips. We were both naked and I ran my hand down her back and over her ass and the side of her thigh—skin, then coiled hair, then skin. She twisted so her back was to me and I felt the weight of her breasts, her ribs, her stomach as I moved my fingers down again, gorging on her neck but not with my teeth, like a horse or a solemn idiot, her familiar body stranger because I knew it now.

"You should have just come here with me last summer," she said later.

"You never really asked me to do that."

"That's like saying I can't understand how you feel because you don't speak Spanish."

"What?"

"It's not even bullshit, it's just . . . I don't even know what that is. I would have done it for you."

"You didn't want to do it."

"You weren't going anywhere."

I didn't say anything.

"You weren't. You really weren't. And I wasn't just going somewhere. I was coming here."

The room's huge windows opened out directly onto the vast square of the Zócalo, with its Mexican flag bigger than any flag I'd ever seen. In the gray morning light, the view filled the black iron frame like one of those balcony paintings of Paris by Caillebotte. It was of a piece with the hotel's lobby and its stained glass ceiling, the bellmen at the entrance in long red coats and top hats. The hotel was like a dream you walked into and the dream was of the afterlife—the vintage elevator, the live birds in cages, the faded emptiness of the marble floors.

I didn't grasp anything about the city's geography and, though I knew it sprawled, it began to seem like one congested highway as we made our way later that morning to where Ana lived with her mother. She was texting someone about work, whatever that meant for her now, and as she tapped at her phone I watched the crowds outside through the cab windows—newsstands, car repair shops, taco stands, cell phone stores—all of it jammed along an endless highway I eventually identified by the street signs as Tlalpan (I will never forget the name Tlalpan because I saw it on so many signs). Ana wore the same clothes as yesterday, as she had repeated her outfits on so many mornings last summer, and it was as if we had just picked up again from there. Trees began to appear between buildings. Then the trees became neatly clipped cylinders and balls and the buildings became low houses with clay-colored or brightly colored stucco walls and thick iron security gates entirely covering the entrances and the garages. Ana and her mother lived on a quiet lane with no traffic, no one on the sidewalks lined with freshly mown strips of grass. We got out of the cab and she punched a code into the panel by the gate. When it opened, there was a small overgrown courtyard with flowers whose names I didn't know, stalks of ginger and bamboo, some plastic chairs, and a table with a watering can on it. I'd had no idea what to expect and what I saw didn't register much—candid, a little sloppy, like my own house, I supposed, which made me feel less, not more, comfortable there.

We came in through a sliding glass door into the foyer, then a dim musty living room full of objects that Ana or her mother must have brought from Venezuela. There was a statue of St. Michael with his wings and sword, one foot resting on the vanquished dragon. There were two of those rotating towers you see in drugstores for displaying sunglasses, spray-painted black, all the slots filled with different kinds of sunglasses, only all the lenses were blacked out and painted over with weirdly colored fluorescent eyes. When we found Ana's mother in the living room, she looked disoriented, as though we'd woken her up from a night spent sleeping on the couch, where she hunched now with her hands planted on the cushions at her sides. The TV was on and she was naked, except for a pair of men's shorts, her bare skin almost translucent in the stale light. The sight of her fallen breasts and gaunt veined arms caused me to look up at her gray disheveled hair, dramatically cut as though with garden shears into a thick brush, hair so striking that it almost made more of an impression on me than her nakedness. Ana said something in Spanish that sounded more like concern than alarm, then more like frustration. She was trying to tell her mother to cover herself, I guessed—there was a blanket tangled up beneath her on the couch. On the coffee table sat an empty glass, books, an empty wine bottle. Ana turned away for a moment, and I was doing my best not to look, and then suddenly Ana's mother was attempting to stand, lurching upward, and that was when I saw the damp stain on her shorts. She hobbled forward and Ana trailed behind her, still trying to sound rational, as they moved out of my sight into the kitchen. I stood there amid the rustic devotional sculptures, like finger puppets carved crudely out of wood, a gold mannequin with a missing head, a sacred heart with flames rising forth from the top, and then I heard a shattering crash and went to see what had happened. Ana was trying to drape her mother with a bedsheet she'd pulled out of the washer-dryer on the far wall. There was a broken pot on the floor, some scattered flowers and blobs of water. They kept struggling with each other until I finally pulled them apart, Ana's mother groaning, her naked shoulders in my hands as I clenched her from behind. She kicked and thrashed, nothing on but that pair of Bermuda shorts, a windowpane plaid of orange and brown, the crotch damp with urine. I hadn't even been introduced to her yet, she had no idea who I was.

I heard the shower come on in the back part of the house, old pipes clanking and juddering in the walls, and I remembered that time I'd spent with Stephon in the basement of the family's house after Jesse's hearing, wanting a cigarette. There was something about families I could never penetrate. I had to take a piss now, and as I looked for a second bathroom down the hall, I thought of an etching by William Blake, which I thought of every now and then. It showed three tiny figures against a night sky, one of them extending a ladder all the way to the moon while the other two watched from a timid distance. The climber's essence was reduced to two words—*I want! I want!*—and it had never been clear to me if the words were meant to be sarcastic or sad or an actual celebration of desire. Given the length of his ladder and the feminine attributes of the moon, it might also have just been a dirty joke. I began to think it was all those things at once, as I stood there pissing in Ana's mother's bathroom.

The line outside Frida Kahlo's house was as long as Ana said it would be when she finally told me she needed some time to get her mother together, so I gave up and walked back toward the main plaza, where we planned to meet later. What I'd just seen at Ana's house was more broken and dreary than I'd expected, and I didn't know if she saw it that way or it had just become familiar. I still didn't know much about her, and this not knowing still didn't change anything for me. I thought of a certain pair of red orthopedic boots Frida Kahlo had decorated with scorpions and sacred birds, another pair ornamented with the hammer and sickle and the Soviet star, talismans against the physical pain that began every day for her as she dressed, magnified to contain the whole world. Malika would have waited in the long line to see the house. One of the things I liked about Malika was how she wouldn't have given a shit about anyone's scorn for Kahlo's popularity. She would have called her "Frida," not "Kahlo." But there was also more to it than that. She used to suspect I had a secret contempt for her art because it was figurative, like Kahlo's, not abstract, like mine—her art was political, not some exercise in "pure" painting. It was about something, not about nothing, as she sometimes liked to say. She thought I disdained the "something," and I would say she was projecting and she would say maybe I was the one projecting, maybe she didn't doubt the value of what she made as much as I thought she did, and maybe the projection went further, maybe instead of seeing her as the person she really was I just saw whatever I imagined her to be. She wanted to make money, was frank about it, and whenever I revealed any ambivalence about making money, she would get irritated because for her money meant power in a world designed to disempower her. It became personal, about being Black, which she said would always be beyond my ken, because although I was some sort of brown I would never be Black. I was thinking about this now outside Frida Kahlo's house, about what Malika would think of me standing there, making a variation of the same error all over again, she would say, imagining Ana instead of really seeing her or truly knowing her.

I had wandered around the neighborhood and the main plaza for an hour or so, when Ana phoned and said I should come back to the house. Then she told me what happened: her sister-in-law had left Ana's mother alone last night, not realizing that Ana wasn't coming home. She said that Ana's mother had already gone to bed and it seemed pointless to just keep sitting there by herself watching TV when she could go home and watch TV in her own bed.

"It's a long story," Ana said. "But she's lying. Obviously. She just didn't give a shit, as usual. There was no money in it for her, among other things."

"It sounds bad."

"There's a woman who helps us, Estrella, she's here now, actually. I knew she'd be here by now. I honestly wasn't thinking this could happen. She's not usually wandering around the house naked."

"I'll come over if you want me to come over, but it seems crazy there right now."

"Let me call you back in one minute."

"Ana."

"I think Hernan is here. Give me just one minute."

We all ended up later sitting at an outside table at one of the restaurants that surrounded the plaza, all of us pretending that nothing had happened. Ana's mother—her name was Consuelo, she had introduced herself now—wore dark glasses and a quilted jacket, though it felt warm out to me. Olive drab umbrellas kept us partly in shade, partly in sun. Consuelo had been a freelance textbook writer and translator for more than twenty years, she needed to tell me, until the internet destroyed the business. They were trying to do everything on Google Translate now, she said, which meant that students got textbooks that were basically almost gibberish, and I said something uninteresting about how capitalism was an engine of stupidity, all you had to do was look at the president of my country. Ana sat beside me, sternly engaged with her phone. Her brother, Hernan, had used the restroom but now he came back from inside, a small man with a neat beard, graying hair, his striped dress shirt untucked over ravaged jeans and black leather high-tops. Families: I didn't like them because I never had one of my own, but also because no family could sit together without an undercurrent of exclusion. I made things worse by bringing up a memorial I'd seen while walking around the plaza as I waited for them to arrive, a display of photographs of young men, more than forty of them, who had disappeared and presumably been murdered on their way from a teachers' college in the countryside to a demonstration in Mexico City. Maybe the closest analogy would be bringing up the subject of police shootings in the U.S. before a mixed crowd of Black and white people.

"For us, it's kind of hard to know how much we really get to feel about that," Hernan finally said.

"I'm just trying to get a clue," I said.

"I travel a lot for work, but I've never been anywhere near there, Iguala, or Ayotzinapa, that's the college's name. It's like a teachers' college with a little bit of the Peace Corps added in."

"I followed it a little," I said.

"Organic farming, history, left politics."

He seemed doubtful that I knew anything about it, though in his defense I knew almost nothing about anything, his own country, Venezuela, being just one of many examples. We talked our way through the meeting points of our knowledge, which meant we talked as much about the U.S. and Venezuela as we did about Mexico. There was a historic massacre of student protesters in 1968, in Mexico City, in a neighborhood called Tlatelolco. The students from Ayotzinapa were going to a march in Mexico City to commemorate the anniversary of this massacre, making an annual pilgrimage to Tlatelolco, where centuries before the Spanish had defeated the Aztecs in the final battle of the Conquest. A lot of blood and a lot of symbolism marked the site, in other words, all of it embodied by the Catholic church built there from the stones of the razed Aztec temple. Unfortunately, Hernan said, Tlatelolco had a very specific meaning for the current ruling party and the army, both of whom had perpetrated the 1968 massacre, slaughtering hundreds of peaceful protesters, most of them students, like the young men from Ayotzinapa. The march was a big fuck-you to certain people, was how he put it. You couldn't talk about the current ruling party or the army without talking about the drug cartels, with whom they colluded in many complicated ways, and this collusion and this history came together when the students from Ayotzinapa commandeered several buses bound for Mexico City, as they did every year in an accepted and peaceful routine, not knowing that two of them contained millions of dollars' worth of heroin in their luggage compartments.

"I didn't think people in the U.S. followed any of this," he said.

"A little."

"The problem is that it's just like a cycle now. It keeps happening over and over—demonstrations, massacres. It's hard to say if people want actual change, or just a theory or a fantasy."

"The problem is that anything that isn't money has no value," Consuelo said.

She started talking in a way I didn't quite understand about some presidential candidate who'd recently gone on TV with a fake book he claimed to have written. An actual fake book, she said, with a fake cover and everything. It was not even a good prop, it looked exactly like a fake book.

"I guess maybe I'm just more willing than you are to admit that money is important," Hernan finally said.

Somehow through all this I could glean that he didn't

entirely share his mother's contempt for the candidate with the fake book, a center-right business-friendly candidate.

"*¿Sabes qué?*" Ana said. "*Ninguno de nosotros puede votar.*"

This made Hernan stop talking. She'd said, guess what, none of us can vote.

Exiles, I supposed you could call them. Not immigrants, not refugees, but something less voluntary than expatriates. Emigrés, maybe. The food began to arrive—a grilled baby octopus, like a charred starfish on a bed of clover-shaped greens, chicken in black mole garnished with a rosette of pink onions. Hernan was in the wine business, so each of them had a glass of white wine from Chile. I declined out of habit but with a surprising sense that I was no longer myself, as if I were as displaced as them, lost in my own theory or fantasy of how life should proceed.

I shouldn't have come, I thought. I didn't know why I had or what I hoped to resolve there.

"I feel like I just got a window into things I didn't understand," I said later in my hotel.

"What do you want to understand?"

"That's not what I meant."

"Do you think I like living with my mother?"

"I guess the question is why do you?"

"It's obvious why."

"My mother was one of those women who always looked younger than she was. She kept her age a secret. She would try to keep it a secret that she had a son, that I existed, and she tried to keep her past a secret, despite her accent."

"I'm not your mother."

"I'm just saying I got a feeling today that I haven't had in a long time, that I don't want to have."

"You'd like it better if I was making a living selling wine to millionaires, like Hernan."

"I'm not trying to make things literal and dull. But maybe I'm wondering how inevitable that is."

10

A few days later, we flew to a city I'd never heard of until then, about three hundred and fifty kilometers north of the capital, where Ana had come to do some work she hadn't told me much about. After a long drive from the airport at night through nothing, then through a clogged neighborhood of improvised shops and food stalls under stark lights, we descended into what looked like a mining tunnel—the city had once had the second-largest silver mine in the world—and drove underground through a warren of streets with staircases at various points for entering and exiting, a kind of catacomb whose timelessness evoked men with black-smeared faces carrying lanterns, mules pulling carts of coal, but also the complicated stone fortifications that surround the Old City of Jerusalem, which did not look much older than these walls. When we came back up aboveground, there was a floodlit palace like something the Medicis might have built in Florence, then narrow streets with bronze posts that kept cars from parking on the sidewalks. Floodlights raked the narrow lanes, the buildings' stucco walls painted in every kind of color, splotched here and there with shreds of old wheat-pasted posters. We hardly talked in the cab. We had not been alone enough for the last several days, dealing with Ana's family, and in the quiet of the dark passenger seat we had our first chance to process it. At the border, ICE had been separating thousands of parents and children from Guatemala, Honduras, El Salvador. Ana had told me her father grew up in rural Venezuela the son of schoolteachers in a dirt-floored hut built of palm fronds, then a small house in the village where the floor was concrete and the walls asbestos. He became a government minister after military school. They always lived beyond their means. He died in Patagonia in an accident on a dove-hunting trip when Ana was a teenager, leaving investments in the Chilean vineyards that boomed after the fall of Pinochet, oil holdings, and two life insurance policies in U.S. dollars. As she told me all this, my country's government was detaining and torturing thousands of parents and children made refugees by its past interventions in their countries' governments. I felt certain that my mother had voted for the president—my immigrant mother who thought of herself as an American. My trip here began to seem unlikely and random. The driver told us he couldn't go any farther into the historic city because cars weren't allowed, so we got out with our bags and stood for a while before the baroque basilica and he explained how to continue to our hotel on foot. Our flight had been hours late. We were exhausted and dirty. When we got to our room, we took showers and lay there on the clean sheets with no clothes on and Ana made me watch part of a movie on her laptop.

For about twenty years, she'd told me before we left Mexico City, her mother had been involved with another woman in Caracas whom she would refer to only as a "friend," even though everyone knew they were lovers, and after Ana and her brothers and their families left Venezuela, the two women practically lived together, from what Ana heard. The lover would probably take care of her mother, in other words, if Consuelo would just bring her to Mexico City, but she wouldn't do this. (The shame had to do with class difference as well as homophobia, Ana explained.) Since their relationship was meant to be a secret, it could be discussed only in signals, which was the tension Ana and her mother had been living in together, both wanting independence, not to mention an escape from the repetition of their past as parent and child. Her mother had told Ana she was thinking of moving back to Caracas, to her old apartment. There was no such thing as safety, she said, reminding Ana of the earthquake that had destroyed her apartment building and caused them to be living together in the first place.

She asked if I wanted to get high and I said I wasn't in the mood. She never wanted to talk about the job she was here for, but when she had to name it, which became unavoidable, she told me it was a podcast, she was making a bilingual podcast funded by a tech millionaire from Nicaragua. It had something to do with people who had left their home countries in the Americas—North, South, and Central—whose stories did not fit into the usual paradigms the audience expected. She wanted to make one about herself, but couldn't do it without upsetting her family more than she was willing to. Her father's rise, her mother's resentment—the irony of her mother voting for his rival, the socialist who became a quasi dictator, partly out of liberal convictions but partly to spite the memory of her unhappy marriage. Ana had voted for him too. Even Hernan had. They thought it would be for the good of the country, which it was for some people, though not for them.

The movie Ana wanted to watch on her laptop was called *El Santo and the Mummies of Guanajuato*, something she remembered from childhood, when she watched a lot of Mexican TV, but it was also connected to the present because Guanajuato was the name of the city we'd just arrived in. Present, past—time seemed to have complicated itself as soon as I arrived in Mexico, distorting whatever I saw or heard, almost none of which I understood, which amplified the sense of its importance. El Santo wore a silver mask because in addition to being an actor he was also a lucha libre star. The Guanajuato

El Santo movie had been blocked on YouTube, so we watched a different one centered on the abduction of teenagers—a fistfight outside a school, a struggle in a car, Manson-like weirdness in a bland Mexican suburb—the acting not only bad but deliberately bad, as if they feared the movie might actually be frightening if they didn't sabotage it. I could see how it would make Ana nostalgic. The El Santo movie had been made in the '70s, before her conscious childhood and only in the earliest part of mine, and what triggered the nostalgia might have been not only the kitsch factor but a certain menace that had to do with the way teenagers in the '70s dressed—like runaways, or the kind of rock stars that used downers, or the kind of rock fans that smoked angel dust—corroded remnants of the '60s swirling into the comic book flavor of the movie to produce a specific tang you could know about only if you had lived in a certain narrow time period that can never exist again. It was like tasting some sort of cheap candy that no one had tried in three decades. It wasn't even that it tasted good, it just tasted like that time period.

"Well, you get the point," she finally said, when I got restless. "You're tired of hearing me translate every single sentence of this."

Her mother was still on our minds, that was why we were watching the movie.

"You were a tomboy," I said, changing the subject.

"What?"

"Or maybe not so much a tomboy as that I bet you had a lot of male friends when you were a teenager. Maybe more male friends than female."

"I went to a girls' school."

"I bet you had a nasty vocabulary. Listened to harsh music like Diamanda Galás and smoked cigarettes, that kind of thing."

"It was the time of Swatches. Guess Jeans. I had a Versace dress, actually, but it was a tame one, black and gold, nothing crazy. You wouldn't have liked me."

"You probably wouldn't have looked at me."

"We would stay out till four in the morning dancing. All dressed up, even though it was mostly just girls dancing with girls, boys slapping each other's backs in little groups. For a while, gasoline was cheaper than water, it was ridiculous. Of course, it was all predicated on the people in the *cerros* who could never dream of putting gas in a car they owned. But arepas . . . They're like balls of corn flour, fried in oil. The arepa you had at four a.m. after a night like that in high school. It was *paraíso*."

"No arepas in Mexico?"

"Of course. But they're not the same. You can't get them like that anywhere in the world anymore, not even in Caracas. Maybe in a thousand years."

"Science fiction arepas."

"Two thousand."

"Maybe sooner."

"I doubt it."

"Maybe in your lifetime."

"I'm not holding my breath. All this talk just makes it seem like nothing, like TV, but I had a life there, an adult life, and then I had to leave. It's dangerous to do the kind of journalism in Mexico I did there, especially for a woman. You might say you get that, but then you act like I'm this rich girl who's too helpless to have her own apartment."

"I never said that."

"I don't have any money. There's no secret there. I have my family. You saw what that's like."

When she left the next morning for her podcast interview, I walked the length of the old part of town, not really knowing where I was going, then made my way back through the thick traffic into a shabby neighborhood of pushcarts, homeless men, tortilla stalls, women's underwear on bargain tables. There was something in the soil of Guanajuato that preserved dead bodies—mummies actually existed there. Some of them were kept in a museum in the hills, which I'd visited earlier, thinking it might be funny, something Ana and I might laugh about, but it wasn't like that. It was a long series of dimly lit galleries full of petrified corpses, like wood, displayed in glass cases. There was the pregnant mummy, the child mummy, the mummified twins. You had to keep walking from one case to the next, because they were arrayed along a hallway that allowed circulation in only one direction so you couldn't turn back. Their faces were contorted in agonized screams, as if they'd been buried alive, or they hunched to one side in a self-pitying groan. I had a memory of myself at Malika's funeral, standing in a dark suit in the humid heat of the church, off to one side of the pew, alone, and it was as if some erasure or blankness in myself had followed me from that moment to now, the hallway going on and on until I had to stop looking—I couldn't imagine how anyone would not stop looking. As I walked back through town now, I saw a man carrying a load of cargo on his head, another sharpening knives on a grinding wheel. There was a shirtless man building a coffin out of wood on the tiny showroom floor of a coffin store. It was hot out and I was dripping with sweat by the time I reached the basilica with its saffron yellow walls and red dome, and I felt a mild achiness, my legs and feet sore. I went inside the church and sat in the cool air of the nave before the gilded Virgin, who held her newly born son in her arms. I never liked to travel because of the sense of my conspicuousness, but maybe I was not conspicuous but invisible—I was the only one in the church, staring at the altar, the saints in their niches, and I thought of the centuries of people who'd sat there before me, whose language I didn't speak, who couldn't see me, though I felt their stares. I remembered the first day Ana and I had met at the café in her old neighborhood, and how we got high after not seeing the art gallery and then took a taxi to Chapultepec Park, where there was a kind of novelty train that took you up to the top of the huge hill where the emperor Maximilian had built his palace in the 1860s. From the terraces you could see the whole city beyond the vast forest and the precipitous drop down the cliff before you. The roof gardens with their boxwoods and poinsettias seemed surreally tranquil compared to the view of the cliff, which I couldn't look at without getting vertigo, that odd mix of fear and desire to lose your footing and fall off the edge.

Ana found me later sitting on a bench in the shade of the main square reading a magazine and I guess I looked tired because she told me I looked strange. She didn't say it jokingly. She put her hand on my face, then massaged the edge of my eyebrow with her fingertip.

"*Quedate tranquilo,*" she said. "You're getting sick, I think."

"Maybe a little. A little not myself."

"It was a good interview. He wants to have us over for dinner."

"Who?"

"Curtis. The man in the podcast. Are you feeling okay?"

"I'm fine."

"That magazine is in Spanish."

"It's more about the pictures. Maybe I am getting a little sick."

"It's okay. I still get sick here sometimes, it just happens. You don't think about bacteria, but the whole thing is basically bacteria. Your entire life better or worse because of some tiny things you can't even see."

It hit me that night just as we were about to have dinner and I had to rush back to the hotel. I couldn't sleep, and though Ana kept insisting I drink water, I couldn't take in more than a few sips before I'd get sick again, and that was how the night went on. The city lent itself to dreams, even if you were awake. We'd spent a few hours just walking around it that afternoon, circling from the saffron basilica to the central garden with its bandshell and cafés, mariachis standing in the shade of orange trees whose leaves, pruned into a rectangular hedge, made a half tunnel over the musicians' heads and the tiles under their white boots. There was a market with a clock tower and arcades designed by Gustave Eiffel, and we took a back way there, a maze of stone stairways between stone houses on the steep hillside that I entered again now as I lay in bed, my stomach bloated, my skin clammy from cold sweat. I saw again the tiny empty square hidden in some corner of the labyrinth—the font built into the wall, the figure of the Virgin—but I was not with Ana anymore, I was on my own, and no one met my gaze, as though shunning me, as though the women wore veils and the men's mouths were covered by the scarf-like lengths of their head wraps. The sun began to set, or maybe there was an eclipse, and there was the sense of receding further in time, past the rose petals and glitter outside the thresholds of closed-up houses, litter left in piles. I turned on my side and wrapped myself tighter in the sheet, then kicked my feet out to the dry air. I saw my mother as she appeared the last time I visited her at the house she lived in with her wealthy new husband, where they talked about chemical weapons in Iraq, which they still believed existed. It was definitely an eclipse, you could tell by the gray light on the stone alleys winding through the houses and gates, the burro with the blanket and harness waiting by the wall not a burro but a donkey, the beast on whose back the Judge would enter Jerusalem. I had never remembered visiting this ancient city with my mother until now, lying in bed next to Ana, where I couldn't tell if the memory was real or just felt real, the street signs not in Hebrew but Arabic, a car veering around the blind corner shouting curses, my mother jerking me up by the arm out of the way, hurting my shoulder, cursing me as I retched again and she pulled me by the arm so we could continue up the winding stairs of the ancient hill.

We were supposed to leave on a flight the next day but after that night there was no way I was ready to travel, and when I told Ana to go ahead without me, she didn't even acknowledge it, she just got on the phone and changed our reservations, haggling with the hotel for an extra night, losing, then calling all around town without success until she found a small house that was available but only for five nights at a time. I told her to go get my credit card but she used her own. I asked her what she was going to do about her mother and she told me she would work it out, there was a difference between important and urgent. What was urgent was that we get our bags packed now and see if I could get myself to the rental house, which couldn't be reached by cab, only on foot, up that steep zigzagging path that I had dreamed of last night while lying there awake. We both had duffel bags over our shoulders as we made the walk, and I thought again of my mother, what it might be like to be my mother's age, sore and nauseated, putting one foot in front of the other in the white heat, climbing the hillside, barely able to breathe.

I managed to stand and wash myself in the shower. I had purged everything from my stomach, but my stomach kept spasming, and the more dehydrated I got, the more sore and flu-like my whole body felt. I told Ana about my dream, how it was suffused with a memory of a trip my mother and I might have made or might not have made to an Arab city in Israel whose winding stone paths looked so much like those of Guanajuato. I thought I could even remember the food on that trip, I told Ana, but I knew this had to be a false memory. Falsely or not, I also remembered the service in the restaurant being slow and hostile because we were Jews speaking Hebrew, but I couldn't remember what man my mother had come to visit—not my birth father, I somehow knew in the dream or the memory. The only thing that made sense about any of it was the way Guanajuato's winding paths resembled so many of those in Israel's ancient cities, like Nazareth, or the Old City of Jerusalem, or my memory or imagination of those real or mythical places.

The last time I saw my mother, I told Ana, was with her new husband, a retired judge in Phoenix who held coarse, inflexible views about politics, which he followed exhaustively. He thought Israel had a historical right to the West Bank, which he called Judea and Samaria. He thought Al Qaeda was smuggling nuclear weapons through drug tunnels across the Mexican border. My mother had been a dancer (I must have still been dazed when I told Ana all this, I think now). She performed with Alvin Ailey for a while, and taught in his school, and she had kept her dancer's physique, which her new husband visibly kept looking at. When we first came to America, I told Ana, my mother dated men of color almost exclusively, which even as a child I saw as odd, a complex. A lot of men lived with us in my childhood, and we lived with a lot of men. I don't know what happened between them and my mother, I only know what happened to me. Fighting off a man who was your "father figure," a thick-faced bearded man who kissed you with sour lips, never stopped being confusing, I said. I never told my mother about any of that. Whenever I did tell anyone, later, I felt the listener wondering if I had really "fought him off" or if I was lying, and then it felt as if I really was lying. I sometimes wasn't sure if I was lying or not. I wondered if my mother's new husband knew anything about her past, her prior life, including the story of my birth father. I didn't expect to like him, or for him to like me, but nothing prepared me for the empty coldness that came from my mother that night, as if she didn't think I was entirely real anymore. It was like she'd become another person, or rather her neoconservative husband had freed her to become the person she'd been all along, an arrogant frightened person who'd finally given up any urge to be better. I'm pretty sure she thought my leaving early was a sign of my instability, not hers.

All the sleep I'd missed the night before now came back in an irresistible current, the pillow and the covers more a part of my body than something outside it. I dozed off for most of the afternoon. Ana came back with a bag of limes and a large papaya and I just stared at her. There was no way I could even think about eating that, I said, and she told me she knew, but this was what I had to eat as soon I could, this was what would make me heal.

"I've been lower than this," I said. "It's just been a long time."

"Don't joke. Do you remember those things last summer? All over my feet?"

"Chiggers."

"I remember I was crying."

"That was the night we talked about Malika. When I told you that whole story."

I'd barely seen any of the house yet because I'd been confined to the bedroom and the toilet, but it felt good to be clean and wrapped up in the sheets where I'd been saying all these things to Ana. I was starting to feel a little better, and when I felt a little better than that I would try to eat some of the papaya she had brought me from the market. We don't get to choose, Malika would say whenever I spoke badly to her of my mother, whom she never met. You don't get to choose the kind of people you fall in love with, it just happens, and if it works out it's not because you made a good choice, it's just because you got lucky.

The underground tunnels beneath the baroque city reminded me of the surrealist Bruno Schulz for some reason, as did the labyrinth of winding paths that made a back way to the market. I think Schulz would have liked the Teatro Juárez with its green, gray, and pink stonework that rhymed with the two palaces farther down the hill. I never saw in person the remnants of the mural Schulz painted in Drohobycz before he was shot to death as part of some game between two Nazi Gestapo officers. I'd told Ana that if she met my mother, she'd probably think she was German—rigid, precise, that kind of thing—and Ana said she had no idea what I meant by that. There were three domed churches just beyond the patio of the little rented house, the nearest with three domes just to itself. At night, music would start in the garden at sunset and sometimes go till dawn, loud choruses of singers, fireworks as startling as cannon shots. There was a funicular that sent up a little red car full of people that passed right by the edge of our patio, like some futuristic amusement park ride. After a few days, we got used to the view of the three domed churches—when we looked at them we immediately pictured the ordinary bustle of restaurants and cars we knew was there but was invisible from that angle and distance. The world was going on, we just weren't thinking about it.

It was still sunny out when we got to Curtis's house—Curtis, the man Ana had interviewed for her podcast. His house, which was really more like a hacienda, had sat empty for decades until he came back for it a few months before the last presidential election, Ana told me, fearing or foreseeing what would happen, a Black man living at the time in Texas. He'd spent most of his life in the States, but this was his childhood home, the place he'd lived in until his parents split up, when he moved with his mother to Michigan. He arrived there speaking only Spanish, an alien among kids of every race and background. The house didn't look like much from outside, where a white gate and entryway stood just a yard or two back from the dusty road, but the gate opened into a kind of crumbled paradise of dry fountains and ragged flower beds, a swimming pool with leaves scattered about the water's surface, an enormous backyard where weeds and high grass grew up around a long wrought-iron table covered with a batik cloth—yellow, white, blue—and place settings and bottles of wine. Curtis wore a cream-colored guayabera that looked serious in a governmental way, not ironic. He was a doctor, Ana had told me. It struck me then why she might have bonded with him. His face and mine, because of our eyes, had the same unconscious suggestion of gravity. Our hair was a similar frazzle of charcoal and gray. His skin was darker than mine but not by a lot. I didn't have a beard but I also didn't shave much, and Curtis's beard was like the fruition of my stubble, not a bush but tight biblical coils. Ana must have told him I was a painter—I never would have told him that—and he asked me about New York, saying he'd lived there in the '80s and hung around with some artists back then I might have known.

"The glory days," he said, after we went through the names. "Maybe a little before your time. Like right before your time."

"Basquiat."

"He was definitely there."

"He was kind of a hard act to follow. Especially if you were interested in all the same things."

"He had a band. I wasn't in it, but I knew those guys. I used to play bass in this and that punk band, this and that art rock kind of band."

His wife, Carlotta, came out, a Mexican woman with straight black hair highlighted at the tips, a pink blouse, loose gold bracelets on her wrists. She shook my hand and apologized for her English, which was almost perfect, like Ana's.

"We'll give you some decent food," she said. "The food in Guanajuato is not the best, I'm afraid."

"He's a vegetarian," said Ana. "He has no sense of good or bad."

"Maybe a sense of right and wrong," Carlotta said.

"We've been growing a lot of vegetables," Curtis said. "I'm kind of into it. I'd like to grow corn, I think it would be amazing to see that, but mostly now it's about different kinds of lettuces. Many different lettuces. Some tomatoes. I'll show you around if you want."

I was feeling better, not achy, and I had waves of feeling almost normal, a little swell of vitality that would fizzle out into a hollowness in my stomach, then go neutral. Curtis told me more of his story while we walked. He worked as a radiologist for a group in Texas, he said—two weeks on, two off—but the internet made it possible to do it right here from home. He went up north for a meeting only once in a while, then headed back straight to the airport—in and out—making money there but keeping it and spending it here. He and Carlotta, who was a surgical nurse, had set up a medical clinic in the countryside where they gave free health care and immunizations to people. A friend of his brought a team of surgeons over every January. He took me through the vegetable garden, a large enclosed space with not only many lettuces and tomato plants, but squash, carrots, beans, high flowering stems of Jerusalem artichokes, herbs, a few fig trees. His parents had built this place in the '50s because they were not only civil rights activists but Communists. He laughed, saying he used to get beaten up in school every day here in Mexico because they thought he was Black, then in Michigan he got beaten up every day because they thought he was Mexican. I smiled and said I went through something kind of similar when I moved to the States, which it turned out I did at around the same age he did. He asked if I'd really been born in Israel: the old story, which I told him. My father was a Tunisian refugee, I said, an Arabic-speaking Jew forced from his home after the Arab-Israeli War. My mother's parents fled Poland to start a three-thousand-year-old life in an ancient language, Hebrew, they didn't even know how to speak yet. They left everything they knew because of a faith they barely practiced but which categorized them as a race. My father was a second-class citizen in Israel, as he'd been in Tunisia, marginalized in both places. We let the conversation slide then and walked back toward the house, where Ana and Carlotta sat at the table on the lawn drinking wine, and he stopped short in the high grass, cocking his head back a little. He was cupping a joint in his hand and was asking me if I wanted to light it up, and since I'd been smoking a little with Ana since I got to Mexico I said yes.

He exhaled, making a sputtering sound with his lips. "I like living here," he said. "I'm not trying to make a huge statement with it. I was born here, I grew up here, but it's not like Mexico has it all figured out, that's for sure."

"I wouldn't be alive if there wasn't such a thing as Israel," I said. "But I'm not Israeli in a way anyone there would even recognize."

"Too American."

"I don't know, is that what I am? I guess it depends on what you mean by 'am.'"

The sun set by the time we had dinner, stretching great cotton-ball clouds of white and pale orange across the sky, the canopy higher here in the mountains than on the Island, with its wide low dome above the ocean. Curtis was making what he called the national drink, the bandera, which consisted of three shots—white tequila, lime juice, and a tomato-based liquid called sangrita—the colors of the Mexican flag. I was high and so at peace that I could take a peculiar pleasure in saying no when he offered to pour me one. We had eggplant salad, goat cheese with little toasts. Carlotta's five-year-old daughter from her first marriage came out to join us. She could count to thirty in Spanish, English, and Nahuatl. She spoke to her mother in Spanish and to Curtis in English. Ana leaned her head against my shoulder and we listened to the daughter tell us a story about a goat who ate someone's clothes. The light beyond the trees had turned the wet gray of new cement. People grew different lettuces in their gardens. Carlotta's daughter's favorite meal was olives and the Mexican cheese called quesillo.

11

had applied for a check-in program through the government called Global Entry before I left, thinking I might be traveling to Mexico more than once and wanting to avoid the lines. They told me I could complete the process with a brief interview when I arrived at JFK from Mexico City, but when I asked the Customs and Border Protection agent how to proceed, he looked at me as if I were asking for something extraordinary, even secret. He made a phone call and told me to go all the way to the end of the building, past the many lines of people waiting to get through passport control, to a glassed-in office I could barely see. On my way there, another Customs and Border Protection agent accosted me and asked where I was going, and when I explained I was looking for the Global Entry office he asked for my passport, which he confiscated before I quite realized I'd offered it to him. I asked him what was going on and he said, follow me. The glassed-in office turned out to be a familiar space, the space of plastic seats and linoleum floors with a cop at a podium in the front whom you stared at while waiting to be booked into jail. I had paid for this service. The agent spoke to the agent at the podium in a voice low enough that I couldn't hear it, then he took my passport to a back room where I couldn't see anything at all. I asked the other agent what he was doing and he said they would call me, but wouldn't say what they were investigating about me or why. I sat in a plastic chair with a few dejected and frightened people as diverse as the world. The Customs and Border Protection agents had provocative dark blue uniforms with epaulets and badges, as if it were wartime. Nothing happened for longer than I could tolerate. I knew they could detain me here as long as they wanted, which was not my fear but a fact, because I was still in the extra-judicial space of Customs and Borders. Eventually I walked up to the podium like the privileged person I was, signaling it with my body in subtle codes that no one could consciously explain. I didn't want to wait anymore, I said, I would do the interview some other time, I would like my passport back. The way I said it made it happen, but it didn't stop the burning inside; it was only the beginning of a long period of burning.

I invited my friend Jerome and his daughter Tyla over for dinner a few nights after I got back, trying to pull myself out of the funk. In the afternoon, Jerome and I went clamming in the inlet above the reservation and we did well, raking up a large bucketful in less than an hour while someone's hired pilot parked a helicopter in the distance, then left a brilliant quiet that made everything twice as vivid: the bands of wet gray sand, the striated clouds, the deep evergreen color of the reeds, and the duck blind like a tattered haystack. I washed the clams in my backyard with the hose, then blasted them all again to get the blades of grass off, unable to resist counting them, admiring the size of the hoard now that it was back in its bucket, then I blasted the patio and furniture with the hose to clear off the oak pollen. Tyla had just finished her sophomore year of college. She had Jerome's round face with traces of her mother in her eyes—Kumiko, who had passed away a few years ago, a rambunctious person who ran away from Tokyo as a teenager—"defected," she used to say—on a school trip to New York City. I steamed the clams with lots of garlic and tomatoes, steamed a bunch of asparagus, which was in season, didn't need anything on it, just some lemon juice, and then I sautéed three soft-shell crabs in butter after soaking them in milk and dredging them with flour, salt, and pepper. I liked cooking as long as it didn't involve a recipe or any skill. Jerome had put on Lee Morgan's "Search for the New Land," maybe with tongue in cheek, and we could still hear it on the outdoor speakers when I brought out the food. It was neither cold out nor hot. The shoots of my daylilies, like folded swords, had grown to their full height, still taller than the flower stalks, which had just put out their buds. The oak trees seemed to loom there with their spread branches as if surveilling us. Ana and I had decided we were going to try to figure it out over the long term. In the meantime, she would visit me here, I would visit her there, we wouldn't rush, we would let things resolve themselves organically, whatever that meant.

"They still haven't cut down those woods," Jerome said. "You're lucky."

"It's not even good to say that," I answered. "That's like an evil-eye kind of statement."

"Maybe they can't subdivide the lot. Probably not, or they would have done it already. You should go in and check the plat."

"I already did. It all belongs to some family who's never here and if they sell it, it can't be subdivided, unless they decide to make a big legal thing out of it. Who knows what happens then."

"You have voles."

"I know I have voles. I have mice. Raccoons."

"These clams came out of the bay?" Tyla asked.

"They're clean," Jerome said. "You're fine."

"What about the lake down there?" she asked. "Do people actually fish in that?"

"Yes," I said. "Believe it or not, I saw someone pull a bass out of there, almost thirty inches long."

"How deep does it get?"

"Like forty feet maybe in the middle."

"That'd freak me out. You swim in there?"

"All the time. I haven't swum in it this year yet, but it's coming. It's happening any day now."

"That's very interesting," said Jerome. "You seen all this on the news? What was it like down there? Tyla's friend is down there. Down there right now at the border."

"Pon," Tyla said. "That's a whole story."

"I wasn't anywhere near the border," I said. "People asked about the president, what was my feeling about the president, but they've got their own election coming up, they're worried about violence, security, gas prices . . ."

I let it drift off, hearing how it sounded.

Her friend Pon was of Cambodian heritage, Tyla explained—her name was short for Ponleu. Pon's mother had been born in a refugee camp in Vietnam that was not under the jurisdiction of either country, and her mother, after more than forty years, had just lost her green card status. She could be deported now, except maybe she couldn't be, Tyla said, because they wouldn't know where to send her. She'd never set foot in Cambodia her whole life. Maybe they'd have to send her back to Louisiana, Tyla said, where they'd placed her family after the refugee camp.

"Cambodia to Louisiana," I said.

"Vietnam."

"Right."

"I guess the thought was that Louisiana is just like Vietnam. A former French colony. Catholic. They eat rice. Shrimp."

"So that's why her friend Pon is down there in Texas right now," Jerome said. "Handing out waters and diapers and medicine outside the bus station. I guess they give people bus tickets to get them to a safe house or something where they can wait till their court case comes up."

"Who?"

"The refugees. Put them on a bus with a bus ticket. Before that, they keep them locked up in holding pens made out of chain link fence inside what's basically a giant empty Walmart."

"Your friend Pon is the same age as you?" I asked Tyla.

"Pretty much."

"It's impressive. I know that's not why she's doing it, but it is."

"Don't start with that Parkland bullshit," Tyla said. "'These young people are so inspiring, they're the ones that are going to change the world.' The world should have changed a long time ago. I'm sorry I said 'bullshit.' It's the right word, though."

Jerome was cutting his asparagus, so habituated to his daughter's thoughts that he didn't have to listen. She went in and put on another record, *Olé Coltrane*, following the thread of her father's humor, knowing about the music because he had played it for her, playing it at my house now because her father and I were old friends, lending each other records.

She left after dinner, taking Jerome's truck to go meet some people. He and I were going to watch a basketball game and then I'd drive him home—I didn't have TV, so we had to walk to the bar a few blocks south of me on the main road. The route took us from my front yard to a dirt lane through a patch of woods where the darkness—the sense that you had entered a forgotten, unseen place—forced both of us to use the flashlights on our phones to see even a few steps ahead of us. We came out of that rural nowhere onto a block of bungalows and shacks used as rooming houses, then we had to walk on the gravel shoulder of the main road as the cars and trucks careened by with headlights blaring with the urgency of an action movie. Almost every year different owners took over the bar, which had once been an Italian restaurant and once even a New Orleans–themed restaurant but was lately, no matter who owned it, just a tavern next to an auto repair stop. It was always busy with different groups of people: men who worked for the fire department, Latin Americans and West Indians who came to watch soccer, young people who turned it into a hip-hop club for a night. Tonight was mostly white kids who had come to sing karaoke rather than watch the basketball game, and the music was so blaring that Jerome and I couldn't talk and for some reason kept squinting as we waited at the bar for his beer and my pint glass of club soda.

It was game four of the NBA Finals, the Warriors leading

the Cavs three games to none, about to sweep. We took our drinks to the back room, where the only table facing a TV was so long it sat almost twenty people, though we had it to ourselves. We both still wanted Cleveland, which meant we came prepared that night to watch without enjoying. We hardly ever talked deeply about our personal lives, even when Kumiko was dying, it was not that kind of friendship, so it was surprising when Jerome asked sometime in the first quarter about Ana and me. I wasn't sure how much he really wanted to know, and instead of wanting to find out I envisioned us from far away, flatter and smaller than we really were, two men at a huge table in front of a televised game, and this image became more ambiguous as we sat there.

"I don't know," I finally said. "All I know is that she's not ever coming back to live here."

"The last I knew she was up here trying to find work because she couldn't find work there."

"I'm not sure what the story is with that."

"It's kind of an important story."

"I don't know, her family . . . You're right, it's important, but it's not something we talk about much."

"You're thinking of moving there?"

"I keep thinking that if I can get it to stop sounding as crazy as that just sounded, then I'll know what I want to do. But I guess I'll also know what to do if I can't get it to stop sounding that crazy."

There were things I wasn't going to say because I didn't want to look at them too clearly. When I encouraged Ana with her podcast, for example, it was the first time I ever felt like I was lying to her. This triggered an irrational image of Ana pregnant with my baby. I had never wanted to have a child and still didn't, but some part of me yearned to have one with Ana when I thought about the podcast, a physical desire, almost sexual, a new fact I had to get used to, which I never told her about.

Four young women, overdressed as if for a rock show, were playing pool at the table next to where we sat. One of them I now recognized as my neighbor Diana's daughter, whose name I could never remember. She acted sheepish about my presence there, turning away each time I tried to make eye contact, then a young man in a yellow hoodie and a black ski cap came stomping in toward the pool table and shouted "Iguodala-a-a!" holding his beer glass like the end of a cane, leaning back and howling in his long black shorts. The way he screamed *Iguodala* made it clear he didn't follow basketball, that he'd just heard of Andre Iguodala tonight by seeing him make some plays and liked the way it felt to shout out the syllables of his name. He kept doing it, usually out by the bar, where the karaoke continued. Iguodala had a big night off the bench for Golden State.

Diana's daughter, whose name I now remembered was Leslie, finally acknowledged me when the shot she had lined up forced her to stand right next to me and Jerome at our table.

"How have you been?" I said. She was lingering near enough to me that to fill in the pause I stretched out my arm to give her a loose, awkward air hug.

"You were gone for a few weeks," she said. "Your truck never moved."

"I was in Mexico for a while. This is my friend Jerome. Jerome, Leslie. Her mother's my next-door neighbor."

They nodded at each other, Leslie not someone he would shake hands with because she was as young as Tyla, dressed only in a ripped black tank top, ripped jeans, her bangs cut in a diagonal slash barely above her eyes.

"I'm actually your next-door neighbor, too, now," she said. "Me and Darren, we're living with my mom for a while. Saving up money. I know, I know how it sounds. Like the dumbest choice anyone ever made. Or the most predictable choice anyone ever made. I want to go back to school, though. I want to be a veterinarian. I always wanted to be that."

"That's great," I said. "That's not dumb at all."

She looked at Jerome, disappointed. She seemed to be asking him if I thought she was just too stupid to talk to, or what.

The boyfriend, Darren, came back in, singing deliberately out of tune to the song about being halfway there, living on a prayer.

"It's off the chain tonight," he said, with hysterical deejay eyes. "It's like an orgy in here, like some place Kanye would be."

"We don't have any cigarettes," Leslie said.

One of her friends gave Darren one of hers, after he pleaded for a while. They'd been playing pool the whole time, taking Leslie's shots for her. The game on TV no longer seemed quite real, as if we were watching a videotape of something that had happened the day before, and it was finally dawning on me that Darren was the same kid who stole the car last fall and crashed it in the woods with Leslie in it. He stood there now with his head a little tilted back, as if taking in a confusing breeze, while Leslie stared at him. I'd gotten an email from Malika's brother Jesse a few days ago, after I got back from visiting Ana in Mexico. *I know this woman you're seeing must be the real thing or you wouldn't have told me about it,* it said. *I was gonna say send me a picture, then I realized that's kind of fucked up. But send me some pictures of Mexico at least. I have a friend who went to Niger with the Peace Corps (I know, could have been me, right?) but I never made it any farther away than Georgia.*

"It's a good look for you," Leslie said to Darren now. "Really helps me to see you bum a cigarette when I have to quit. When you know I have to quit."

He looked like one of those people who got a tiny taste of consequences after crashing a stolen car and then immediately forgot that trouble still remained a possibility in his life, a charming kid with a cleft in his stubbled chin and sarcastic eyes. Even Diana had forgiven him—Diana, who'd come to my door that night last fall in tears at the exact same moment Jesse called me from prison to tell me about a friend who'd been beaten to death in a two-man cell.

12

My phone was on when Ana texted, saying she wanted to Skype, even though it was very late, so I logged on to see her face obscured in shadow, then asked her to turn a lamp on, then to turn it back off because of the glare. There was no sign anything was wrong until she told me she'd been digging through old boxes and found some copies of a book she'd published a long time ago, a stack of identical thin volumes she showed me now by angling her laptop toward it. The feed paused and caught up with itself in that occasional stop motion that accentuated people's gestures, making them almost like animated renderings of themselves. Her book was about a neighborhood in Caracas, she said, 23 de Enero, and how by tracking the changes in that single place you could depict the history of Venezuela from the '50s boom to the crisis now. She showed me the frontispiece, a photograph of huge housing blocks, interspersed with serpentine stretches of shanties and a few sprigs of green space. Her producer at the podcast didn't really understand her story about Curtis, she told me. She wanted less about Curtis and his family and their two generations of exile and more about the medical clinic—more poor people, Ana said, more "sad," because sad made people comfortable. It preserved their belief in otherness, their own distance and innocence, made them feel virtuous without having to do anything. She'd been a real journalist once, she said, profiling politicians and artists and celebrities, but also reporting on serious stories, like this little book about a neighborhood in Caracas that many people she knew would be afraid to even set foot in. The podcast, the diminished career, her problems with money—she told me about all these things before she told me she'd been pregnant with our child for a few weeks, until two days ago, when she miscarried.

Her gaze met the screen with less force than actual eye contact but the wavering image had the solemn quality of candlelight during a blackout.

"I was too old," she finally said. "I mean, also I was on birth control. At least I thought so. But as soon as I found out, I knew that probably nothing would come of it. That's why I didn't say anything to you."

She was trying to spare me from a loss I didn't feel, even though I think she knew I didn't feel it.

"It won't sink in for a while," she said. "Or maybe it won't at all. I never expected to feel like this."

"Like what?"

"Like this helpless desire to keep it alive."

She looked at me through the screen, weathering some sort of shame, then faintly shook her head.

"It's ridiculous, I know. I can't really even picture it, actually. Also, there's a difference between wanting to keep it and wanting to have it. It was barely even an embryo. Like a little cell cluster."

"I can picture it," I said.

"I don't think you'd even be able to see it."

"I can see it. I understand, though, why you didn't say anything."

It was after midnight when I went out on the water, moving through tangible darkness, the pond's shape like the mouth of a volcano, no sound, no color, only grays and blacks. I steered from the boat's rear seat because there was no wind, and this enabled me to imagine I was pushing an empty gondola, or maybe not a gondola but the barge Charon poled across the river to the underworld. The faint moon, almost entirely covered by thick clouds, left a darkness so intense it was hard to believe I'd be able to see even a few feet in front of me, but every time I pushed forward the light spread a little farther, I saw more and more of the water. It wasn't that I was indifferent about the miscarriage, it was that I had to face once again a void inside myself that I wasn't going to try to understand anymore—it was an absence, not a presence, not something you could understand. I remembered when my artist friend Lucien had had his first child, many years ago, he couldn't hide the fact that he didn't want it, that he dreaded it—it was not something he could say, but you could read it in his face, and every time I asked him how he felt, he met my eyes with a dead gaze and silence, which took a certain amount of self-confidence, I saw now. I didn't feel that way, but I also didn't feel any ping of joy when I imagined having a child. The difference now was that we knew the world was ending, the genocides and fires and thousand-year floods already here, not in some abstract future. I reached a spit of land with a high stand of cattails, then turned, and even at the edge of the pond where the trees cast an unbroken band of pitch-black shadow, I could always move through the barrier, it opened up as I approached and I would see more light in front of me, then a little more.

It was starting to rain. I didn't mind, it was as diffuse as a mist, but as I started cutting back across the wide body of the pond it came on a little harder. If the wind kicked up I would not be able to steer, I wouldn't have enough torque, and

I'd be stuck out where I was, a hundred or so yards offshore, but I still didn't mind. Thousands of drops hit the water and kept hitting it, like bullets falling straight down, and if you looked through the scrim to the other shore it was like one of those fireworks that keeps blooming outward with streams of silver. It rained that hard for only a minute or two—by the time I reached the midpoint back to the dock it was just a mist again. I kept paddling. It was so dark in the shadows cast by the woods that it wasn't until I was about twenty feet away that I saw the figure out on the platform, less than a silhouette, a vague black form against a darker blackness.

It was Darren. He ashed a cigarette into the water. Even when I got close enough to grab the edge of the dock and pull myself in, I couldn't see his features. I told him not to put the butt in the lake and he told me he wouldn't do that. People did it, I told him. Left them on the dock, tossed them in the water, whatever. The dock was destroyed from the winter freeze—I'd been meaning to fix it—the main platform halfway underwater, some planks missing, weeds growing in the sediment of mud. I stepped out of the boat onto the walkway, which was shaky, but stable enough to stand on. Darren put his cigarette between his teeth and helped me yank the boat out of the water and walk it back up the slope into the patch of white pines where I stored it.

"I would never put a cigarette out in the lake," he said. "Know that."

"Okay."

"Seriously. I come down here to be discreet. I didn't mean to spook you out just now."

I knew how furtive he felt sitting on the edge of the dock in the middle of the night with a cigarette. I knew because I was out there in the dark too.

"Leslie told me about you," he said.

"That doesn't sound good."

"I know who you are, in other words."

"And who is that?"

"She said google you and I googled you."

"Right."

"So now I know more about you than I know about people I actually know."

We were standing on one of the steps that led down to the pond, a rounded length of pine wedged into the dirt of the hill, where we were protected from the drizzle by the tree canopy. He told me he had some friends who'd ended up becoming tattoo artists, because that was the way for someone who liked to draw and paint to make money now—the only way for the kind of people he knew. He didn't have any tattoos, he said. He actually still hated needles, even after all this time. He told me a story about a hemorrhoid he got right at the beginning of his last detox—it was the mother of all hemorrhoids, he said, like a hard rubber ball bulging out of the side of his asshole, caused by the constipation that sometimes went along with opioid use, and he never felt such excruciating pain, even in the detox itself. It was the fear of another hemorrhoid like that that had enabled him to actually quit, he said. He told me about being bent over a kind of table while a surgeon and his resident cut away at his rectum, and when they were halfway through they came to a spot that the anesthetic failed to reach, and the pain of that was like a lighter flame, unforgettable. Suboxone, he said. Every morning he put two strips of Suboxone under his tongue until they dissolved, which gave him the tiniest little bit of a high but kept the craving in check, though it also made him want to smoke cigarettes even more than before. He wondered if it was true that I didn't make art anymore—most people wouldn't want to stop or even be able to, he thought—and we both made a few observations, none very true, about the correlation between quitting drugs and quitting painting.

"You can use the boat," I said. "I mean, not now, but whenever. I'll leave the paddle out here. At night, it's like white noise. Or like watching fractals on a screen."

"Fractals. I haven't thought of those in ages. It's like the end of the world out here, it's so dark. Or like the world already ended. Like that heaven-is-a-place-where-nothing-ever-happens song. You're a thing. You were a thing. Why are you talking to me like this?"

"What do you mean, a thing?"

"A person you can google and find out about."

"Rabbit-skin glue. You wanted to know why I quit painting, and the way I always try to describe it is to say that it had something to do with rabbit-skin glue. It's what you use to prepare a canvas, it helps the paint adhere, and also it stretches the fabric when it dries so you get a better surface. People have been doing it for centuries, smearing the rendered collagen of rabbits on a rectangle of fabric so they can paint pictures on it. I just thought that was basically the essence of everything that was wrong with me. I didn't even prepare the canvases myself, I had an assistant do it, and that made it worse. It was like I'd spent my whole life making whalebone corsets. Being a juggler on the sidewalk. It was even stupider than that, because I took it very seriously—you have to take it seriously, like you're doing heart surgery, if you're going to do it at all. People paid thousands of dollars for it. More than open heart surgery costs. Rectangles of canvas smeared with rabbit-skin glue and paint. I didn't know who was stupider, them or me."

I told him I had to go, it was late, and I reminded him that he could use the boat whenever he wanted.

"Sit still, I know," he said. "Get your thoughts together, that's the move. Also, float tanks. You sit in the tank in the dark and it kind of resets everything. It's expensive though, I think."

"You'll be all right," I said.

I said this, but I knew that being all right for people like Darren and me could be like fasting for your whole life, then like fasting for your whole life while holding your breath.

13

It was easy to spot Ana outside the arrivals gate at JFK because she wore a rose-patterned huipil (I saw now that she wore huipiles more in the States than in Mexico). She looked distant, or maybe I just imagined she did. I put her bags in the little back compartment in my truck and we started the long drive east—in spite of our smiles and the few mild jokes there was a coldness between us, and this feeling intensified as I entered the five o'clock traffic where I had to focus on the frustrations of driving, moving into lanes, blocking the way of others, not on Ana. I had brought her some fruit and a Gatorade and a bottle of water, and I could see her sitting next to me with the Ziploc bag of cantaloupe in her lap, tired, then finally she put her hand on my thigh as we moved slowly down the Long Island Expressway, past bland towns invisible except for the green signs naming them. She made a joke that instead of splurging for a night in the city I was just driving her back to my house, where I'd probably make a primitive dinner instead of taking her to a restaurant. She didn't want to stop, not even for the bathroom in Manorville, and when we turned onto County Road 39 the clouds stretched out in thin bands the color of the cut-up cantaloupe in Ana's bag. We'd been driving for three hours, the sun almost all the way down, when I made the mistake near the reservation of taking the scenic route, turning left at the traffic light at the college where I taught. The narrow road led through the golf course and country club named for the tribe whose former land it stood on, a groomed landscape of grass and sand with views like in Scotland that went all the way down to the bay. This wasn't the mistake. The mistake came when we got to the long, winding road around the pond near my house. The view then was the view of last summer: silver glints of water through the shadowed limbs of trees. It brought home that in the space of a year we'd gone from strangers living across a patch of woods, Ana still casually dabbling with her friend, my neighbor Jack, to this moment when it felt as though our entire lives had been compressed into the dark cabin of the truck.

She didn't want to come into the house. I turned off the ignition and then the headlights and we stared at the walkway lit by a Chinese-style lamp on either side of the front door, the silhouetted bushes still, as if on purpose.

"Do you remember that little plastic turtle?" she said. "We were so upset because we thought it was dead. I don't know why I'm so tense right now. *Preocupada.*"

"It's the place," I said.

"Like Curtis's place, except without the people."

"I never quite saw it that way, but yes, I guess."

"I'm just saying how it felt."

She was staring at me in a way I began to realize was no longer judgmental but more like she was just struggling to see me clearly. She brought her face closer to mine, until it was too close to see, and we started kissing. Strands of her hair were in my mouth when she pulled away, the truck like something left on the side of the highway that you glimpse in the weeds and wonder about as you pass by.

I shucked some oysters at the glass table outside while she showered in the outdoor shower. The moon was out and music came faintly but unpleasantly from Diana's house, the beat and cymbals of party time.

"You feeling okay?" I asked.

She nodded as she walked across the lawn, wrapped in her towel. "Your neighbors are louder now."

"There's more of them."

"It is beautiful here, though. Outside, at least. It really is."

She leaned her head back and took in the night sky, which I couldn't see from where I was because of the torches I'd lit. Even Ana was hard to see as she brought back one of her feet and twisted a little on the lawn like a dancer, or like someone pretending to dance. The air was warm and still and she stood there with her head tilted back, hugging herself not because it was cold but because she was letting it sink in, where she was.

"These trees," she said. "They're so still, they look like they're being patient. Is there corn?"

"Not yet. It's not quite ready yet."

"I remember that corn. It's so sweet. It's like a drug."

The humidity rose the next day but the sky remained a deep blue, and when we went to the beach the ocean under the bright sun was clear and green like the Mediterranean. I dropped her off at the road's dead end with bags full of food and drinks and another bag of towels, then I drove back to the hospital, where it was free to park, then I walked back past the rich people's houses to rejoin her. To understand how many of those houses stood on each of those blocks and how those blocks spread for miles, all the way to the tip of the Island, was to understand how many thousands of people had so much money they could afford not to fear the end of the world. I walked back to the beach in the shade of the trees that formed deliberate alleys on either side of the street, and I saw the bags Ana had left for me to carry, then I saw the ocean, the specific size of the waves always surprising, like the soft crushing sound of their powerful force breaking on the sand. I wondered which way she had gone, knowing she would already be lying down on the blanket, to my left or my right, in the same black bikini she wore last year.

She had lived here long enough that summer that she had a doctor, a gynecologist, whom she'd seen before and whom we visited that Friday. It wasn't like some TV commercial where I went with Ana into the office and we tearfully held hands while the doctor described our options. She went in by herself and I sat in the large light-filled waiting room staring at the art on the walls, which was surprisingly good, abstract paintings whose loud colors were modulated by thick slashing brushstrokes the black of Japanese or Chinese calligraphy. The memory of my old paintings in Lucien's loft left me faintly nauseated. Lucien had come around in the end. He'd hated the nights of screaming and feeding and changing diapers, but eventually he became a good father to his daughter and later he had two more kids. I had no way of understanding how that happened. We didn't discuss it because we had never discussed his previous aversion. Ana came back from the consulting room and gave me a skeptical shrug.

"I have to go over to the hospital to have some bloodwork done," she said.

Her comfort food in this part of the world was a Malaysian dish called roti canai, a very oily flatbread served with thick brown gravy over meat or chickpeas. We ordered one of those and a vegetable dish. The restaurant was in an old bank building and had a sweet formality to it—white tablecloths, waiters dressed in black—that made you feel as if you'd gone to a different state, not just the next town over, which somehow made it easier to talk. There were some things to think about, she said, although my part in them still felt ambiguous to me. She didn't know if she even wanted to try to get pregnant again, but she had to make up her mind soon. Most people her age, the doctor told her, ended up needing help. She advised Ana to go to a reproductive endocrinologist, who would look at her bloodwork and do some additional tests. The inhibin test she had just ordered at the hospital would tell us if her eggs were normal or more fertile than was usual for her age (there was some reason to think this because of the pregnancy she'd just had). In either case, she could take an oral medicine called Clomid, which increased ovulation, but it would probably not be enough help, and the first decision she would have to make was if she wanted to waste time trying the Clomid or go straight to IVF. The doctor asked Ana if she really wanted to have a newborn baby at her age, if she had really thought about what that even meant.

"I don't know if I know the answer to that," she said.

"Nobody does."

"I remember the earthquake. Being afraid to die, obviously. Thinking I was definitely going to die, then when I didn't, being so relieved, it was like everything had a new level of realness. The sidewalk, the jacaranda trees, all the people out there. The idea of pants instead of skirts, the idea of sandals. Stacking floor after floor of a building made out of bricks and concrete and trees. You see where I'm going."

"What do you want to do?"

"I guess I just want to see what happens."

"With the bloodwork?"

"No, in general. A huge effort would make it less of a long shot, but not a sure thing. Not even close. It's like climate change that way. The doctor said you have to know where your line in the sand is. She said that at my age there's a good chance I would have to buy donor eggs. Did you know a donor egg costs twenty thousand dollars? I didn't know that. She said sometimes people get together and pool their money to buy eggs from the same woman, split the cost. It's a crazy road. The minute she started telling me about buying eggs, I saw that."

It was a relief when the first course came and she started eating, tearing off chunks of the roti and dipping them in the sauce. It was all precious, was what she was saying about her neighborhood after the earthquake. Also, that it was one thing to not want children, but another thing to feel you'd lost one.

14

'd removed what I thought were all of Malika's things from the house, but I'd held on to some that we'd both owned—paintings mostly, most of them by friends—and sometimes I couldn't remember how various objects came into my or our lives. Her souvenirs—the folk art made out of mirrors and tin cans, the Dogon mask—I'd put in boxes and sent to her sister, Sherril, and to her mother and Stephon, where I imagined them in the garage with the other boxes and broken electronics and unplayed musical instruments. In the gaps on the walls, I'd left either nothing or put other paintings and drawings by friends, the result occupying space without coherence or the sense that a human person actually lived there. I hadn't realized the old clutter had coherence. One of the things I had a hard time getting rid of was the big red rug with the Zulu patterns that covered the living room floor, which I'd lived with for so long I didn't even see it anymore. It didn't remind me of Malika, it was just a part of the house, which Malika had never even seen, but it had been her rug, and it upset me to roll it up and put it in the back of my truck and donate it to one of the charity thrift stores in town. The living room floor when Ana arrived from Mexico was just bare pine planks, glaring in its nakedness. In a closet in an extra bedroom I never used, I still had some of Malika's clothes, either from Africa or in African design, their brilliant colors hard to deal with, the blues and golds and reds. I was hoping the college would include the clothes as part of an archive it already had of some of Malika's art and studio artifacts, but in the meantime, after Ana and I went to the hospital, I put them in the back of my truck and drove them to my office on campus, where I stored them. It felt like severing my last tie to Malika's living presence. When I took the dresses and shawls out of the closet and put them in my truck, Ana wasn't there.

Diana invited us over for a barbecue that Saturday. I had been down looking at the dock, measuring how much wood I needed to replace and seeing if I also had to replace the poles, which I'd made a few years ago with conduit pipe, and Diana spotted me as I walked back to my house. Her old boyfriend Sebastian was with her. He bumped fists with me with half-closed eyes, embracing and making fun of the gesture at the same time.

They looked guiltily proud of their happiness, which they'd returned to like a new season on TV, but unlike Ana, they were both willing to get into the mucky pond with me and so we spent a few hours that afternoon loosening the brackets and raising the dock's main platform up on its poles out of the water. The more time we spent together, the more impossible it became to say no to the barbecue. Ana and I went over a little before eight o'clock with a bottle of wine, some club soda, and some chips and salsa I made from scratch (the key was to fry the salsa in a small amount of oil before you boiled it down). A border of trees separated our backyards, which meant we had to walk to the front, where Sebastian used to refinish his furniture, and that was where I saw the parked cars and trucks along our little street, an inevitable indicator of who was going to be there, mostly sailing people, not the preppy kind in polo shirts and leather shoes (though they might have crewed on those people's boats) but locals who knew how to fix engines and put a boat on stands to scrape and paint its bottom for the winter. Tiki torches in the backyard gave off tall flames and plumes of oily black smoke, and sunburned men and women stood around a keg, most of them probably natives of New York or New Jersey, though they wore incongruously tropical shirts, sunglasses hanging from cords around their necks, baseball caps with place-names or brands on the front. The music was neither Jimmy Buffett nor Jack Johnson, but jam band music with classic or southern rock elements, time now not to chill but to get closer to rowdy. I was seeing all this through the lens of someone's truck on the street that had a sticker in the rear window depicting the president of the United States as a mischievous eight-year-old boy gleefully pissing on the word *Democrats*. As I looked at the faces, I knew the truck could have belonged to anyone, and also that my interest in the question of whose it was didn't matter, because in a way it belonged to us all, except maybe Ana. I was glad she didn't notice the sticker, or at least I didn't think so. I came back from the picnic table with some drinks and she'd already found her way to the side of the yard, the side near my house, where she and Diana and Leslie and one of Leslie's friends were laughing. I said hello and they introduced the other young woman, Yoselin, who'd gone to high school with Leslie and now was about to become a senior in college upstate. She spoke an aside to Ana in Spanish, maybe about me, I couldn't tell. Ana told me later she was Salvadoran. An occasional firework boomed or crackled in the distance, which upset the new puppy Leslie held in her arms. She cradled it like a baby and kissed the top of its wrinkly head over and over.

"I want to be like Daisy in my next life," she said.

"You want to be a dog?" asked Yoselin.

"Either a dog or a tiger."

"I'd come back as a ninja."

"Uh, right, macho. Like Uma Thurman in that movie."

"I'd come back as a man," said Diana.

"What?" said Leslie.

"First of all, tigers are an endangered species," Yoselin said. "Why would you want to come back as an endangered species? I'd come back as a man, too. Like just go around and rub my dick all over everything. Blup, blup, blup. Whip it out and go for it. Guys don't need all this prep like we do. They're just like fuck it, I'm getting laid."

"The cutest guy I ever met," Diana said, "was this Greek guy, really dark and chiseled, but I could tell maybe he was gay because he was just too good to be true. It was even worse than that, though, because what he really wanted was to be a woman. 'I want to get me a pussy,' he kept saying. Like over and over. And I was like, why would you want that? You don't know what you're talking about."

I kept thinking about the sticker with the president's image on it, but I also noticed how Ana was enjoying this conversation in a way that surprised me, and I could imagine her later telling me about how there was still something she liked about Americans, how alive they were. She and Yoselin could be present at this party without attracting anything but humor and goodwill. Just by being in the yard, physically present instead of an abstraction, they almost became part of the group, among these descendants of Italian, Irish, Jewish, Polish families, who all believed they were white. My brain was like one of those old TVs where you manually turned the dial to change channels, one station ceding to another with a thunk. I had maybe five stations, and one of them now was a sentimental black-and-white sitcom about a daughter Ana and I might someday have. I didn't know why a daughter and not a son, maybe because I was in a group of all women, and I didn't stay tuned in long enough to figure out anything about the story, if there even was one, and when I thought about it, I realized I couldn't even get to the level of image—it was just an aura, a vague sense of a "show" made of tangled ideas and emotions. I came back to the present to find Leslie and Yoselin performing some sort of transitional sketch, posing with territorial grimness as they chanted *I don't dance now, I make money moves. I ain't gotta dance, I make money moves.*

I was out of club soda, so I walked back to my house, where I didn't find any more. It was dark when I came out onto the street again and someone was walking out of the woods above the pond, taller and more distinct as we got closer to each other. It was Sebastian, who'd been down at the dock and was soaking wet now from a swim.

"She seems cool," he said. "Your friend. Mexico City, I hear it's great there. A lot of people are traveling there these days, it's like a hot spot."

"I liked it but probably it was just because I didn't understand most of what was happening. If you can't speak a language, you can imagine that everything people are saying is interesting. It is interesting, because you can't understand it."

"Kind of like a four year-old."

"I like Diana. You know, that dock down there, it's kind of a funny story. I built that whole big platform on my front lawn, which I was very proud of, but I forgot to think about how I was going to move it from my house all the way down the hill to the pond. It weighed like a thousand pounds. And it was Diana who figured out how to do it. She knew there was a place down the road where you could back a truck up right to the edge of the water, so we managed to get the platform up onto the bed of my truck and tied it in place with some rope and we drove it around. We dragged it in the water, and it floated because it's wood, and I just walked it slowly around the edge of the pond, pushing it like a table on wheels, all the way around the shore, until I got it here, then I bolted it in place."

He was a photographer, he told me. He did lots of shoots for women's magazines, usually in New York, but also all over Europe and the Caribbean. I didn't believe this, but as a lie it was specific, unexpected, and I didn't see any reason for him to say it if it wasn't true. I think he was waiting for me to ask him more about himself, his past, but I wasn't interested in that kind of conversation, the establishment of who'd done what, what merit or appeal they had or didn't have and why and to what extent.

"You get high?" he finally said.

"Just weed once in a while."

"Let's go back and get high."

A truck was coming up the road, bouncing a little on bad shocks so its headlights slashed jarringly on our faces and the trees around us. It turned out not to be a truck, but Darren in the van he drove in his job for the pool company. The vehicles behind him were trucks, two of them that along with Darren's van idled in the road with their lights glaring, as Darren stepped down out of his cab.

"Montauk," he said. "Too much fish. We were throwing back bluefish. Tons of fish."

"Striped bass?" Sebastian asked.

"Striped bass. Black sea bass. Mother ocean's whole bounty."

He gestured with a can of beer he must have been sipping on while driving.

"You text while you drive or just drink beers?" I said.

"Haha. You gotta take some of this fish. Seriously."

"Sure."

"I'll hook you up. Look, I got to tell these guys where they can park. I had like one beer. One and a half. You're going to go out of your way to lecture me for one and a half beers."

We headed back to the party. The breeze kicked up in the woods behind the house, rattling the leaves and drawing the smoke from the tiki torches into long waves. Sebastian passed his vape pen and asked Ana about a photographer in Mexico City who made color portraits of superrich housewives in their ostentatious homes. I couldn't remember if I'd seen these photographs before or not—the red living room with the zebra-skin rug, the rococo mirrors, the woman luxuriating on a leather sofa in a white robe that showed the tops of her breasts—had I seen it or was I just imagining it now from Sebastian's description? The night wore on, people went swimming in the pond, skinny-dipping, coming back dripping and cold, without towels, their clothes back on and soaked. We went home around eleven with a whole bluefish Darren had packed in ice inside a garbage bag. In bed, we could hear fireworks going off over the pond. They must have been shooting them off the dock. It would be the Fourth of July that Wednesday. I liked to sleep with the windows open rather than turn on the AC but the music in Diana's yard kept playing, hip-hop now, Darren and Leslie and Yoselin's music. I fell asleep once I shut the windows, the room so dark you couldn't see the nightstand right next to the bed. I had a dream about a wheelchair basketball game in a crowded high school gymnasium, clusters of fans dressed in matching outfits of yellow and blue shaking pompoms in the bleachers, or eating hot dogs beribboned with ketchup and mustard. A point guard dribbled up the gleaming court in his chair, holding up a fist to call a play, while the others rocked back and forth, poised and waiting. The president of the United States was in the crowd. He sat in the bleachers next to the former president who'd gone to Andover and Yale and liked to spend his weekends clearing brush on his Texas ranch. They both had hot dogs too. The preppy one was pretending to like the taste of his, even to savor it, while the one from Queens sat sullenly not eating, bored and increasingly irritated. The players were war veterans, I understood somehow. The game was part of the aftermath of the wars, except the wars were still going on.

"You always get too high," Ana said, when I told her about it later. "You need to be careful. Take care of your brain."

15

The next day was Sunday. It was hard to tell what was happening next door at Diana's place, because so many people came in and then left, the dock crowded with strangers, maybe Sebastian's friends, people getting high while floating in the water in plastic inner tubes, playing music on portable speakers bluetoothed to their phones. We stayed in my living room and listened to Ana's podcast about Curtis, which they'd finally put online. After the barbecue, I found myself wanting to go somewhere else until the Fourth of July was over, or just wanting the neighborhood empty, the pond to myself. The main theme of Ana's podcast was the precariousness of "home," how space could collide with time to erase our lives and transform us into people we never would have recognized. It reminded me of that book by Baldwin I'd read with

Jesse last year, who by then had spent more than two decades in prison. *Time passes and passes. It passes backward and it passes forward and it carries you along, and no one in the whole wide world knows more about time than this: it is carrying you through an element you do not understand into an element you will not remember.* We were listening to the podcast on Ana's laptop, lying together on the couch, her body on top of mine, her head on my chest. I wondered where all those people at Diana's could be sleeping, because she rented only half the little house, the other half belonging to her landlord, who was almost never home but kept his stuff there. In Ana's idea of home, everyone spoke Spanish, and one of the missions of her podcast was to help people learn the language as a form of cultural connection (this was the Nicaraguan millionaire's conception, but she shared it). Topless bathing was popular with the people at Diana's house, the female ones, and Diana, too, so when I went down for a swim that morning I tried to signal that I noticed but didn't care, that I admired their free spirit and their bodies but not in a gross way, not to the point of desire. Leslie wore not only a full bathing suit but a T-shirt over it. Darren, sandwiched inside a pink raft, promised not to discard any smoking materials into the lake. Curtis spoke now in Spanish about his childhood. I'd never heard him speak Spanish but I recognized his voice, and for some reason the combination struck me as humorous. I told everyone I didn't speak Spanish, but in truth I'd been trying to learn

it ever since Ana left last summer, with an app on my phone
and also online, and though I'd made some progress I could
hardly understand anything Curtis said until Ana translated
it for me. He was telling a story about moving from Mexico to Ann Arbor, Michigan, in the late '60s, where he somehow met Iggy Pop and got Iggy's band to play at his junior
high prom, and then how later Iggy Pop stole Curtis's first
girlfriend. In Ann Arbor, he had tried to watch the Mexico
City Olympics on TV, the 1968 Games where John Carlos and
Tommie Smith raised their fists in solidarity with the rev-
olution, and his mother shut off the set and yelled at him,
because he knew that just a few weeks before the Mexican
government had massacred a crowd of its own citizens and
jailed hundreds more, some of them her friends, at a demonstration in the plaza at Tlatelolco. There was never really any
such thing as "home" for Curtis, he said—Mexico City, Guanajuato, Ann Arbor—each place was so different that it nul-
lified the one before. His mother eventually became famous
for her work as a historian in which, using shipping records,
she built the first database of the names and places of ori-
gin of people kidnapped from Africa during the transatlantic
slave trade. It gave their descendants a way to know where
their ancestors came from, a place-name, not a home exactly
but a homeland, which was a word I wasn't used to hearing
without feeling skepticism, a word Ana understood in a way
I couldn't. We had settled certain things now. I was going to

come with her when she went back to Mexico—I had already bought my flight ticket—and I'd stay there until I had to go back to teaching in the fall, and then I'd try to figure out a way to stay there all the time. It was her home, it mattered to her. I once had a friend who thought the drive to have children was even more powerful than the sex drive, which I always thought was ridiculous, until now, when I'd told Ana that if she wanted to have a child we could try to have a child.

Sebastian and the others left that Monday. Maybe they had to go back to work in the city, though I doubted it was that, because he and Diana had an argument—I could hear faint snatches of it from my back patio—and the crowd left in the morning, as if giving them a chance to reconcile, but Sebastian left in the evening. It was quiet then. In Mexico, they'd just elected a new president, a populist whose ideology no one knew much about, though he won by a landslide because the other choices were so unacceptable. A Nobel laureate from Peru warned of catastrophe, comparing the president-elect to the leader of Venezuela. That was what Ana's brother Hernan feared. She felt nothing in particular. He was better than the president he would replace, she said. He was better than the president here.

On the Fourth of July, I made a version of a bandera without alcohol—small glasses of tomato juice and club soda and cut-up limes, which tasted like it sounds, pointless and disgusting, but we laughed, then we went up to the bay to watch the fireworks. We spread our blanket out not far from the spot last summer where we'd found that abandoned Porsche stranded on the sand. The Fourth of July—I always thought of Kerouac and his Roman candles, or that song by the band X about a marriage breaking up while on the street Mexican kids shot off fireworks. So many people—many of my close friends, as the cliché goes—didn't celebrate the holiday or didn't know how to feel about it. People like my mother and her husband found this kind of position exasperating and absurd. I remembered the moment last summer when Jerome and I saw the car drive into the crowd in Charlottesville, and how he left me there in front of the TV in silence because there were no words for how he felt, and how in that moment we were living in different countries. Ana and I could hear the fireworks in the distance but couldn't see much until later in the show, when big jellyfish shapes opened up the sky, dangling their tentacles down, then shimmered out into embers and smoke. Yellow and silver, red and purple, blinding silver orbs that rose straight up and flamed out at the top of their range. Ana lay on the blanket with her head tilted up to the sky. I used to get questions from students wondering, for example, if Kandinsky's paintings referenced landscape or historical paintings from the past, if all those abstract shapes and blobs got their sense of harmony from the way they echoed compositional conventions, and I would tell them yes, it was obvious, nothing was new. My sense of home had narrowed to a tiny point in space, then an absence or a vacuum. It was time to give up on what was no longer there. I realized this was probably the last time I'd ever sit on this beach and watch the fireworks.

It had been quiet on my street since Sebastian left, but when we got home from the bay that night there was a town police car on the street in front of Diana's house. I noticed the flashing lights as I came up the hill toward my driveway, then after I parked, I turned off the engine and my own headlights, and Ana and I got out of the truck, Ana a little before me, so that I considered how still she was standing and wondered what was wrong. She was listening to Leslie sobbing, which was when I finally heard her myself. I paused for a moment like Ana, then told her to wait for me. I kept thinking there'd been a fire in the house, though there was no fire truck—this was the kind of senseless assumption I clung to as I walked around the trees to the front yard of Diana's house and saw Leslie sitting on the edge of the grass with her feet in the road, bundled up in a huge black T-shirt with the logo of Darren's pool company on it. She was saying something about her mother, the same thing over and over, and it took a long time before I could get her to calm down enough to say more.

"She's in there lying to the police right now," she said.

"What do you mean?"

"She can't keep her hands off her own daughter's boy-friend. Is that normal? My own mother? I've been stuck with this shit my whole life."

I stood there waiting for some wave of clarity that didn't come. Ana had joined us by then. On the other side of the pond, someone was setting off bottle rockets and clusters of tiny firecrackers, and a little later—right before Leslie brought her puppy out and left with her friend Yoselin in Yoselin's car and the police finally drove off—Diana screamed something so loudly from inside the house that we could hear it out on the lawn. It was so jarring and sour and unlike her ordinary voice that it didn't sound real at first, as if she were trying to shake Leslie with the volume of her voice, to shake her into understanding what had really happened.

I saw Diana the next morning when I came back from check-ing my empty mailbox and she was in her driveway packing things into her car. She was leaving to stay with a friend in Pennsylvania for a while, she said, then she apologized for making a scene last night, tears starting in her eyes, which she resisted almost to the point of anger. We didn't know each other well but we were connected by the shared past that goes with being neighbors, like siblings who barely kept in touch. I had never even been inside her house. I took it in now as we walked up the stairs—she asked if we could talk for a minute—and into an apartment that was even smaller than I expected: a kitchenette connected to a kind of nook that served as a living room, built under the eaves of the house so the ceiling slanted down to make it even more cramped, then a bedroom through whose open door I could see the unmade bed. He had assaulted her in here, somewhere. The sight of Diana in that small space with its wicker furniture, curtains made of old bedsheets, flies and unwashed dishes on the kitchen counter, made me imagine her life more clearly. There were wilted plants in macramé pot holders, a tin ashtray that looked vaguely Moroccan, a framed poster of a painting of a peace lily, the kind of possessions she must have had since her twenties, living for boats and the water, time spent in nature.

"Ana must think we're all crazy," she said. "I know you always thought we were all crazy anyway."

"I never thought that." I sat down on the love seat with a glass of water she'd offered me. "It's a meaningless word, anyway, *crazy*. Maybe I wondered a little bit about what you were really like. What mattered to you."

"Leslie was living with her grandmother for most of the last few years. My mother. I thought it might help, that she'd understand better what I went through growing up, because for a long time Leslie and I couldn't be under the same roof together. It just wasn't possible. Oil and water. Or like two animals who wanted to kill each other. Things go in cycles. We had a bad history. But I'm worried now it's over between us. That this is the last straw."

"She'll come back."

"I wanted to ask you a favor."

"What?"

"I wanted to ask if I could text Leslie your phone number. Maybe she'd want to reach out to you. I know that sounds nuts, but she thinks you're some sort of mythical thing. This reclusive artist. She respects you. She won't pick up when I call, but at least she'd have your number if there's an emergency. Or in case she wants to come back here and pick up some more of her stuff."

"Text her the number. Of course."

"But I don't have it. That's the thing. Could you text it to me?"

After years of living as next-door neighbors, we didn't even have each other's phone number. She told me hers and I sent her mine, then she gave me a spare key to her place for while she was away. No one ever believed stories like hers, she told me. When she was fifteen, no one believed her either. She said she didn't expect Leslie to believe her or to ever forgive her—she had seen this all before. Leslie was a dreamer, she said, wanting to be a veterinarian, when she could barely stand working at the pet store in the village. She said Darren used to work on fishing boats—his biological father was a fishing boat captain in Montauk, she knew him, too. The truth was she'd been dating Darren's father for a few months before Darren started dating Leslie.

"His son," she said now of Darren. "That's what you have to imagine. They always say 'animal,' he's an 'animal,' but they just mean he's unreachable. They mean that if he hears you, it just comes across as noise."

16

The dock was still broken. We'd lifted the platform mostly out of the water, but it didn't change the fact that the planks were rotted out and the weeds were still thriving in the gray mud between them. It was lucky no one got hurt, stepping on a nail head or gashing up their feet on the splintered wood. I took off my clothes and got in the water, I didn't care. Something about its smooth faint pressure against the skin as you moved through it never failed to calm me. I swam halfway out, then turned to look back at the shore, at those giant trees that weren't registering anything in terms I could understand. The late morning light spread over their green foliage, laying out a huge reflected sheet, like an undulating mirror, on the pond's surface. Everything was soaked in the bright colors of paint-by-numbers sets, shiny pools of deep lime and fluorescent yellow.

A few beer cans listed in the grass at the pond's edge. I picked them up on my way out of the muck and put my wet body back into my dry shorts and bundled up my shirt and underwear and sandals. Chloe, the neighbor's black poodle, came charging out of the woods, then into the water, then bounded back up on the other side of the dock and stood there panting, waiting for me to come nearer. She barked and I didn't move, barked and I still didn't move, then finally she couldn't help herself and came closer just as I started stepping forward. Her soft coat was already almost dry where it was shaved closest to the skin, and though she wagged her tail she stood very still in front of me, bowing her head slightly like a horse presenting itself for grooming, dignified, not begging. Ana and I were about to leave for the city that afternoon on the bus, I had to get ready soon. She'd set up an interview with a lawyer who represented Mexican clients facing capital charges in the U.S., death penalty cases. He needed someone to interview the families and friends of such people, who were usually indigent and spoke only Spanish, in order to construct a sympathetic narrative to present in court. This was the kind of work she was hoping to get into when we went back to Mexico. I walked hunched over clutching my clothes and phone and those beer cans, dripping wet, onto the path through the woods with Chloe following me. I remembered Darren floating on that pink raft in the pond. I didn't know where he'd gone. I never expected to see him again.

"She's leaving town for a while," I told Ana about Diana when I got to the back patio. "She said she doesn't feel safe here right now."

"Is she all right?"

"I didn't want to ask about it too much but the sense I got was that they aren't going to charge him with anything. Darren, the boyfriend. I just want to get out of here. I keep thinking about that puppy she had. Leslie. Has. It's like it's not one thing after another, it's everything all at the same time."

"Make it stop."

"That's right. Make it stop."

I slept through most of the bus ride and didn't really come out of it until we left the Midtown Tunnel and made the turn up Third Avenue. The streets outside were full of young people importantly oblivious to the others moving from block to block, buying salads before the shimmering glass atria. We took a cab to our hotel on the other side of town near the Lincoln Tunnel, the building renovated to evoke a hip cartoon, retro and futuristic at the same time, like lounge music. You checked yourself in on the ground floor at a series of white computer terminals on a long white counter, a kind of fake airport desk at which you were not only the passenger but also the ticketing agent. When we got to our tiny room, it was decorated like a first-class airplane cabin, the retracted bed covered with a snug blanket, a monsoon shower in a glass enclosure. I could feel the cheerfulness trying to reach me and not quite getting there. The whole city was like a trance I was watching through the clean glass of that shower enclosure.

"It's ironic that Leslie is staying with Yoselin," Ana said, her back to me as she stood at the window. "The Salvadoran friend."

"What made you think of that?"

"This room," she said, still looking outside.

When she left for her interview the next morning, I took the Grand Central Shuttle to the 4 train to Lucien's loft in East Harlem. He wasn't there, that was our arrangement, and though his loft was cluttered as usual in the front, as I went farther in I could feel a certain faint vertigo at the sight of the space he'd emptied out for me, gray and grayly lit like the butcher section of an old grocery store. There was a booklet of text pieces Malika had made for *Darkadia* left on the seat of a yellow chair where he knew I would see it. He knew I would pick it up, that I would sit in the chair thinking of him as I opened it at random and started reading, talk radio playing somewhere in the background, too faint for me to locate its source.

A.: *We just walked in.*

Q.: *What do you mean?*

A.: *We just walked in. Through the back door. They don't*

lock their doors out there. Or if they do it's always something cheap. An antique, or there's a window. It's not very hard to get in.

Q.: They leave their doors unlocked.

A.: They leave their keys in the cars. Hide the house keys under a doormat. It's a part of their privilege, they think. This "freedom" they think they've paid for. I know all about it because I grew up in a place very similar, I was one of those girls. They had TVs everywhere.

Q.: Were you wearing masks?

A.: No.

Q.: No masks.

A.: No, we just wore whatever dark clothes we could get together. When it's hot, the last thing you'd really want to have on is a mask. I wouldn't want to wear anything at all, actually, but we were told to wear clothes.

Q.: Were they asleep when you got there?

A.: No. When we got there, it was only about ten thirty.

Q.: So they weren't asleep.

A.: No.

Q.: Well, they must have been pretty surprised to see you.

A.: Well, this one (laughs). They were surprised, yes. They were all in different rooms. Every single one of them in a different room. I was with the father at first. He was in his little room downstairs. This little home office he had. Once they see you, they can't move, but they try to show you they're angry. You're *"invading their privacy." You just look at this—this little man with his sports magazine. You'd think you'd start laughing at all this, but instead you just get very angry at every little thing you start to notice.*

Q.: So what did you tell him?

A.: I told him, let's go. I told him he was coming into the living room.

Q.: Did he say anything?

A.: He thought I was alone, I guess. You can sort of hear the way they think it sounds. It's like they still have this power. But when they say it, then they hear it. Get out or I'll call the police. *That's when they know it's not what they think it is.*

He'd hung up six of my old paintings on the walls of the main studio, three canvases on either side, everything else in that vault-like space the same grayish white, the floor, ceiling, and walls almost mocking in their well-lit sterility. It was like a stranger had made the paintings, someone who'd scoured away any timid impulse to make light of the situation or be ironic. Romance and nostalgia were killing us, they said. Amnesia was killing us. Hate like a form of masturbation was killing us. The paintings gave off a hum of black light, of secrets and threats. They worked changes on a private language of harsh diagonals, omphalos shapes, railroad grids, snakes, though one of the canvases was all pastel colors, like a speckled cupcake, bright paint crazily hatched onto a white ground that was like thick frosting spread with a rubber spatula. You could taste the overload of sugar, feel the itch of the crystals on your teeth. It triggered tiny talismanic scratchings whose symbolism was undercut by every brushstroke but still there, a stubborn wildness within the rigor, hue laid on hue laid on hue, an electric amp or a rune, a glassine baggie or a piece of beach glass. Bronzes and blacks, aquamarine and blood red, the pink and white and baby-blue stripes of a rep tie from the 1980s—you couldn't disagree with abstract paintings, not if they were any good. They didn't assert any meaning. I'd been afraid to look at these things for almost a decade, even before Malika died, and I saw now that I'd misremembered them completely. I'd lived the wrong life and was still doing so, it was impossible not to, the paintings said. I knew the scene from Malika's *Darkadia* I'd just read morphed into something even uglier: black-and-white images of cut-up bodies, assassination scenes, the faces of Malcolm X and Martin Luther King along with the followers of Charles Manson, whose foreheads were carved with swastikas, no mystery to Malika, for whom they were just an expression of whiteness, turned inward and gnawing on itself and the world.

A.: You can hear the daughter upstairs. Like she's trying very hard to breathe. I mean, she was trying hard to breathe, but nobody'd even laid a finger on her yet. Nobody had touched her. But you could hear this all the way downstairs. Justin came in then. Justin came in and he was moving very fast. He was all in black, and of course he had the gun. He just grabbed the father by the hair and threw him out of the chair. Just threw him across the room. He said, "What do you think is about to happen now?"

I was still in this fog when I encountered Lucien later at the café on Lexington. The talk radio, Malika's text left on the yellow chair—he'd been fucking with me a little, I understood that. He was sitting by himself at a small table, looking at a magazine through bright red reading glasses halfway down his nose. Even in the heat he wore a blue denim shirt, its long sleeves rolled up damply, a trilby hat made of dark straw. When he saw me coming, he kept the magazine in his hands but planted them like fists on the table, glaring up at me like a disapproving librarian, which was how he looked when he was trying to adjust his eyes to see better.

"Elizabeth Catlett," he said, referring to the African American artist who emigrated to Mexico and lived there most of her life.

"You're here," I said. "I thought we'd have at least a few miscommunications just for tradition's sake. Like a text from you saying you're in Brooklyn, where am I?"

"Not your kind of thing, Elizabeth Catlett."

"Elizabeth Catlett. Käthe Kollwitz. They sort of rhyme or something."

"They're both great artists. Great artists." He put the magazine carefully down on the table. "You survived the viewing."

"I'm getting there."

"I'm sure it was a lot. I know exactly what it was like."

"It was all a long time ago."

He nodded, almost yawning, as if my dismissal of the past was too boring to even point out as a lie.

I ordered a coffee and we sat there and talked for a while. He'd been spending a lot more time in Vermont lately, he said, staying up there during his teaching semesters all week and making studies of the night sky. It started with that app on the phone that told you the names of constellations, then he decided to buy a telescope, then a better telescope, a better tripod, all of it crammed into the little house he rented with its wood-burning stove and no TV or computer. To walk out at night in the winter in Vermont he'd bought special snow pants and boots, mittens like oven mitts, face masks, and several of those hats with floppy ear covers stuffed with down. You could be outside in any weather, he said, if you had the right clothes. We'd been friends for more than twenty years but I'd never thought of him as a person who would take to stargazing in a freezing climate, walking around in the woods all night by himself. He liked the challenge of trying to remember what he saw, he said, which at first was practically nothing, as he realized when he thawed himself off in the house and tried to make a sketch. He got better at it, though. It was like learning a language. His girlfriend and his kids would kill him if they knew he sometimes went out there without his phone, headed out into the snow at night with no umbilical cord, which made the walks a completely different experience, profound in a way that became harder to resist once you'd tried it. He could remember a lot more of what he saw now, not just the stars but certain shapes of clouds, the silhouettes of trees whose bare branches had the same jagged graphic quality of the woodcuts of Elizabeth Catlett or Käthe Kollwitz.

"When are you leaving for Mexico?" he asked.

"Soon. I just want to see what it's like to stay there for a while."

"I haven't been back to Jamaica in a long time. Five years, six years. I know I could go back now and feel all right, but it's been a long time, like you said. When I was young, it was not safe. I mean, I'm straight, okay, but they're going to beat you up anyway for being a batty boy if you act like me. Maybe kill you, as a matter of fact."

"I'm going to get those paintings out of your place when I come back."

"That's a good idea. I'm not keeping that space much longer."

"No?"

"I've kept it too long already."

"I thought you had some sort of deal. That you knew the owner of the building or something."

"Your paintings looked good on the walls in there."

"I know what a pain in the ass that was for you. You know I know that."

"How much do you think you can get for them?"

"Haha."

"You remember how much money you used to have?"

"I remember it. I wish I still had it."

17

The line in front of the Shake Shack tightened into a dense mob as the bus came to a stop on Fortieth Street. We stood our ground and got seats near the front, stowing our shared duffel bag in the narrow rack above our heads. Ana's meeting had gone well—the job, as the lawyer described it, paid decent money and would put her skills as a journalist to undeniably valuable use. She would talk to someone about the next step when we got back to Mexico. As we sat there waiting for the bus to pull out, a neurotic man moved slowly down the aisle asking if the person sitting there planned to recline his seat. You could tell that on previous journeys he'd aggressively complained about people reclining, their encroachment on his legroom, and his solution now was to annoy everyone on the bus before we left. We sat and talked about what we would do when we got to Mexico, where we planned to stay with her mother in the house in Coyoacán, which Ana promised was bigger than I realized, almost two houses separated by a courtyard, though with only one kitchen, in the part where her mother lived. She told me her friend Magdalena had offered to give me Spanish lessons—whenever Ana and I tried to speak Spanish together it felt too artificial—if in exchange I would speak conversationally to Magdalena in English. Her English was fine, Ana said, but not good enough for her brother, who lived in Boston, where he played violin for the Philharmonic, and who'd said that Magdalena couldn't come visit him there until she lost any trace of a Mexican accent. He resented how people in Boston treated Mexicans, Ana said, but he was also just a snob.

"I guess it goes with the classical violinist part," I said.

"You're a painter. You're not a snob."

"Not that kind of painter."

"Maybe too much the opposite. Do you even own a suit or a pair of nice shoes? It can be old-school in Mexico."

"You're saying you want me to clean up."

"Have I ever told you anything like that?"

"Not really."

"Not at all. Not, not really."

"Boston's tough. Uptight, racist. It's like those boat shoes."

"He's just a snob."

No matter how much she'd told me about her past, I still didn't have any real picture of it—the Versace dress, the girls' school in Caracas, dancing in her bedroom with rubber O rings on her wrists like Madonna. I guess her family lived like rich people anywhere in the world—Manhattan, Paris, Lagos, Dubai—until they stopped being rich.

On our way home from the bus stop we made a trip to the farm stand, then I drove us through open fields—corn, spinach, potatoes—and into the woods, where the shadows of the tree branches made intricate lattices on the asphalt road and their leaves above blazed in such high contrast that it was almost blinding, hard to steer. Diana's house was empty, no cars in front of it. The neighborhood was not just quiet but essentially abandoned, no one outside. When we got out of the truck, the air felt good on our skin after the bus ride, though it was humid and hot. Whatever bad feelings Ana had when she first arrived here on the plane seemed to have gone away, maybe because we were leaving soon, I was not staying here when she went back to Mexico. If everything worked out with the criminal defense job, she'd told me, she could still do the podcast if she wanted, but she could also let it go—it felt good, she said, to suddenly or at least possibly be in a position to turn work down.

"I need a shower," she said. "I'm disgusting."

She turned on the radio in the living room, reporting from Thailand about a group of boys and their soccer coach who'd been trapped for two weeks in an underground cave, miles from the exit, the escape route mostly underwater because of floods that generated powerful currents in a space of total darkness. We learned now that the previous day, four of the boys had been rescued by divers, who today had just rescued four more, ferrying them through the lightless passageways underwater and over rocks and mud on sled stretchers in the narrow tunnel. We stood there looking at each other, Ana's face frozen in a way that looked mournful but was actually more like Rilke's phrase about every angel being terrifying. Unbelievably, after two weeks of certainty that they would die, they might all be saved.

We wrapped ourselves in towels and then left them on the hooks inside the outdoor shower and stood there naked together waiting for the water to warm up. She put her hand on my chest and we started kissing. The shower had blue slate patio stones for a floor, lined with pale pea gravel, surrounded by bark mesh screening. The water was warm enough now for us to get underneath it and we stood there pressed against each other, still kissing. I crouched down a little, my hands moving from her hips to the outside of her ass to hoist her up, and we stayed that way for a while, until it stopped working, then I pushed the shower head to one side and guided her down to the wet slate floor, where I lay on my back and we kept going while the water poured down. She had gotten her blood test results last week, the inhibin test to see the condition of her eggs, but the only thing it determined was that she should get another test, a different test—the results were that there were no results. Her wet skin in my hands and her small body made me think of a dolphin, which was a way of thinking of mermaids, the otherness of the ocean. I didn't notice I was cutting myself until it was over and then we were both laughing, saying now we really needed to take a shower.

We were leaving in just three days and I would not be here in this otherness—water, trees, sky—that sometimes held more meaning for me in its silence than human language. We had corn cooked on the grill inside its husks, sweet and bicolored, along with some tomatoes from a friend of mine at the college who always grew too many—last year's tomatoes, canned in Ball jars. The light in the backyard seemed to pulsate with the faint sparkly sheen you sometimes got when looking through a soap bubble. It was odd to have no neighbors. I made a red sauce with the tomatoes and ladled it over spiralized zucchini cooked in olive oil. Ana didn't seem to mind the food, which she called "clean," which made it sound like yoga. She had a single glass of wine, drinking it so slowly that I wondered how. I could never have more than a few sips of wine or a cocktail before I started rewarding myself with the idea of another one.

"They saved those boys," she said.

"I know. It's like the opposite of news. It's like a Disney movie."

"I should Skype my mother tonight. Tell her about the job interview. We can talk about those boys in Thailand."

"This corn is where it should be, finally. It just gets better from now on. I always liked living here, but it also always kind of seemed like a mirage or a hallucination. It's like that Borges poem about Adam trying to figure out if he was ever in the Garden of Eden or if he just imagined it or if there was even any difference. Do you know that one?"

"I don't think so."

"It's a good one."

"I'm glad you're learning Spanish."

"A lot of his stuff is not that hard to read in Spanish."

I had an email from Jesse that I saw after I cleaned up the kitchen. He hadn't called since I came back from Mexico, which I thought might be a sign that he thought I was preoccupied, fading out. He hadn't heard from me in a while, he said in his message. He hoped everything was okay and then he said he was reading the Bible again and asked if I ever made it through to the end of the book of Exodus. The whole thing became more like a modern story when you got to the end of Genesis, he wrote, the part about Joseph and his brothers—Joseph's brothers selling him to slave traders because they were so jealous of how much their father, Jacob, favored him, giving him that coat of many colors, and how Joseph ended up a house slave in Egypt. Right away, his master's wife fell in love with him, Jesse said, and when he resisted her she did the usual thing—she accused him of trying to rape her and had him locked up in prison. Very modern—slavery, prison. It made sense when you remembered that the English brought the Bible with them on their ships when they came here. He didn't know how stern Moses was until he read it all over again, how his story began when he killed an overseer for beating a slave. It was such a weird book, he said. Every time there was dramatic action, there would be a long digression about rules—dietary laws, hygienic laws, sumptuary laws—ruining the story, so you could tell some priest had come in later and inserted these passages like an endless commercial break during the Super Bowl on TV.

I understand why you would want to go to Mexico, he wrote. *I mean go there to stay. It got me thinking about how when I get out of here I'll face a totally different world. When I first came to prison, there were no cell phones, no Facebook, barely even any internet. Guys come out of this place and can't figure out how to buy a toothbrush, I'm told, there's too many choices, or you have to order it online. A foreign country, is what I'm talking about. Like you in Mexico. I'm gonna try to keep one foot in and one foot out, you know what I'm saying, to not forget where I came from. It's like when I got to the end of the book of Exodus and there's a lot of drama going on, Moses brings down the Ten Commandments, they're about to cross over into the Promised Land, enemy territory . . . it's really a war is about to set off. And then they stop everything right there and there's maybe five chapters just telling you how they built the tabernacle, this moveable temple with the ark inside it. What kind of architecture there was. What kind of columns they used. The different stones and the types of wood. The ornamentation. They tell you exactly how much gold and silver and bronze they used to build the gates and the doors and the hinges and the altar. Part of the ornamentation was badger skins and ram skins they dyed red. I remember all this because I could really see it. They're trying to paint a picture, make you sit with it for a long time before the story moves forward, take it in. The temple is moveable. They're going to take it with them to the Promised Land, but what they don't realize is that they're already in the Promised Land, the actual arrival is just a matter of time. The whole book of Exodus just ends with this long description of the temple. This was how it looked . . . The End. And I was like, what the fuck, and then I realized why they did it that way. It's because it's not just*

*about some specific piece of land, it's about this other space
that is everywhere.*

I went outside to read on the patio in the light of the camping lanterns so I could feel the air on my skin. Ana had fallen
asleep in the upstairs bedroom after her Skype conversation.
She was wearing a T-shirt of mine from decades ago with a
Basquiat print on the front, a kind of private joke to myself
about my distant origins as a graffiti artist and wannabe. I was
reading Borges in one of those editions that gave the Spanish
original on one side and the English on the other. I tried to
translate it myself without looking at the opposite page. I had
to look up a few words on my phone and also to make some
adjustments beyond the literal word-for-word rendering in order for it to even make grammatical sense.

> *Todas las cosas son palabras del*
> *idioma en que Alguien o Algo, noche y día*
> *escribe esa infinita algarabía*
> *que es la historia del mundo . . .*

I first heard the sounds as whoever it was came around the
trees separating my place from where Diana lived, approach-
ing from around the side of the house where Ana was asleep
in the upstairs bedroom. I thought it might be Sebastian, for

some reason, but then the figure in the dark saw me see him and he paused and I knew it was Darren. I remembered that night down at the dock when I came out of the boat to find him smoking in the darkness, and he must have remembered that night too, because his posture was the same, disarming and self-mocking, and he used the same kind of soothing words, telling me he was sorry, he didn't mean to startle me—"again," he said—with a kind of understood wink, and then he told me he'd come to the front of the house first but could see through the storm door that no one was in there, though the lights were on, so he thought he'd check back here. He wore shorts and mud boots with black socks halfway up his calves, a Hawaiian shirt in a lurid pattern of green, purple, and yellow. When he stepped a little closer into the light, the shirt looked like it had been wrung out and dried after soaking in a ditch. He wasn't staying with Leslie at Yoselin's, he wasn't staying anywhere, he was getting high, I saw. I had put my book down on the table and now I closed it and stood up. He seemed to be trying to get a read on me. Would I respond if he simply asked for help? There was a moment, in other words, when I might have handled all this differently.

"You're like the kid who couldn't get arrested," I said.

"I know. Why is that?"

"Maybe it's that shirt."

"I really thought we were kind of on the same page, you and me. Like addictive personalities, overthinkers, grinding away all the time on the big mysteries, all that. But I know, I know, sometimes I'm too smart for my own good. But sometimes I'm unbelievably dumb. Like right now. I was trying to do this unobtrusively. Not make a scene."

"Where is Leslie?"

"She comes home from Yoselin's and sees us in the kitchen just at the exact moment when we were pretending to flirt with each other. I mean, I like came out of the shower with a towel around my ass and Diana said something like 'nice buns'—some shit from *Three's Company* or something—and that's basically all that really happened."

"You should get out of here," I said. "Obviously."

"I'm just wondering if you have a key to the house, by any chance. All my stuff is in there."

"I don't have a key."

"I'm feeling unbelievably dumb right now. I mean, the whole thing. I can see it all from the other perspective now. I know you have a key, though. Leslie said you did. It's like you'll let me borrow your boat, but I don't need a boat right now, I don't need a hobby. All my stuff is over there."

He moved so fast I could barely discern what he held in his hand, which was a box cutter that slashed across my face. I didn't feel much, just a damp cold on my cheek, another drop of it on my forehead, but then my eye started burning so badly I thought I might have been blinded until I realized it was just closed. He was trying to open the screen door, to get in the house, and I was stooped over with my hand in front of my face afraid to touch anything, frozen in place as if waiting to learn how serious it was. I groped my way around with blood on my face and hand, barely able to see, following Darren into the bright house, madness streaming out of both of us now like the garish tropicalia of his shirt. I heard Ana coming down the stairs and wondered if Darren had known she was here. My burning eye was like nothing I'd ever felt before. I thought maybe Ana had sprayed tear gas, that was how badly it burned. I dove on top of him, trying to take him down, but he was stronger than I thought, and then he stabbed me in the thigh as I was thrusting my knee up into his groin from between his legs. It felt like the blade had jammed itself all the way to the bone, a bruised feeling behind the flame in the muscle. He buckled forward and I brought my elbow down on the back of his neck. All the lamps were on in the living room. I pounded his face into the bare wood of the floor and after that everything started to happen in frames. I pounded again and again. He was on his back, his bloody mouth like the mouth of a caught fish, one of his teeth loose on the ground. I lunged toward the couch, trying to catch my breath, then sat for a moment, then lay down like an image of myself on the lid of my own crypt. Ana wouldn't answer when I called. Darren and I lay there for a long time until I saw the lights through the windows and the clear glass of the storm door, a staggering number of red, white, and blue lights. I was on a stretcher then, outside an ambulance with a pressure bandage over my eye, though I could see some of what was happening around me. Ana was standing in the street with no shoes on in that Basquiat T-shirt, held back by a cop. I didn't know if I was going to the hospital or to jail.

18

Time passes and passes. It passes backward and it passes forward and it carries you along, and no one in the whole wide world knows more about time than this: it is carrying you through an element you do not understand into an element you will not remember.

I remember wanting to leave the U.S.—that's the feeling that stays with me now, much more than the physical pain of my recovery. I remember moving into Jerome's place because I was too distressed to go back into my own house, sleeping in Tyla's bedroom, which was the only one on the ground floor; I couldn't climb stairs or walk at all without crutches. I remember the bewildered gratitude I felt the night the plastic surgeon sutured and dressed my eye (I was fully conscious), then calmly described what would follow. Later, the police detective induced in me a similar sense of defenselessness, though this time swirled with many other things—above all, I did not want to be the kind of person he thought he was there helping. I wasn't in the hospital for long, just one night, then to Jerome's. Ana spent most of the next week at her friend Jack's house. I finally met him, his surprising blandness causing Ana to seem somehow less familiar but not more mysterious. I remember one afternoon, once Jerome and Tyla had left for work, Ana and I tried to have sex in Tyla's small bedroom with its single bed and ironic boy band posters, my leg sore beneath the bandages and brace. It was her time of ovulation and she'd started taking Clomid, which was why we were doing this, despite the absurdity of the place and my condition. From then on, every time we tried to conceive a child it was the best chance we would ever have and maybe the last. I wanted to do what my body wouldn't do. Or maybe it was not my body but my mind. That blur of shame, pain, displacement, sadness is what I think about now when I think about leaving the U.S. forever.

In the parking lot outside the prison, I took out my driver's license and a few twenty-dollar bills and stored everything else in the glove box except for the keys, then I walked squinting over to the reception building in the white heat. After nine months, there was still a strange dry itch from the scar tissue every time I moved my eyelid, which was all the time, but I could see. It had been raining hard when I got to my motel the night before, water puddling half a foot deep on the sidewalks, the sound like millions of quarters poured onto a giant plastic table, but now it was as if none of that had happened. Violence, amnesia—I'd forgotten it could be eighty-five degrees in the South in April, the sky somehow a deep blue while also shining with the heat of the sun as if reflected off the chrome of a car, low cotton-colored clouds rolling over a flat landscape of trees and telephone wires. I'd just sold my house, then flown here to say goodbye.

Inside the waiting room, there were too many people for the small area to hold, so the line to get through security coiled back and forth like an approximation of lines at the airport, more people coming in through the door, letting the hot air in from outside. You stood on the conveyor belt with your shoes in your hands, one in each, and looked down at the spot while they moved you slowly sideways through the X-ray machine. At the end I always felt anxious, something about going through the machine and what it presumed, and I felt a little harried putting my shoes back on and getting myself to the check-in desk to give them Jesse's DOC number so they could print out my pass. How many times had I done this and yet still I was affected by it, the waiting room with the TV playing an old western with John Wayne and Kirk Douglas, the water fountain that didn't work, all the young children waiting with their mothers or grandparents, none of them misbehaving, none of them crying, few of them making any noise at all. You got on a bus, depending on what camp you were going to, and sat in the gray seat for the long drive through farm fields— vegetables and cotton—bordered by perfect white fences and even a few flower beds, all of it strictly groomed by work gangs of men locked up there. Jesse's camp was past the main prison with its sports fields and basketball courts and military-style dorms surrounded by chain link fence and razor wire, a huge world within the huger world. Camp D, it said on my pass, and the driver called out Camp D, and I got out and waited to be buzzed through the sally port, then I handed the woman guard my pass, then I waited to be buzzed out, then I waited outside the steel door of the visiting shed where there was no button to press, no knocker, you just pounded on it until someone finally answered.

I'd already told Jesse about the arrangement I'd made with Darren when he came out of the hospital that summer, how I wouldn't press charges if he went to a rehab facility in Minnesota, which I paid for, and that from then on he had to stay employed and write me an email every day for the next two years. I didn't have to write back unless I wanted to, but he had to keep writing whether I did or not, and if he didn't take it seriously enough I could tell him to write another message, and if he still didn't take it seriously, or if he stopped writing altogether, I had the option to press charges for two more years, which was when the statute of limitations ran out on assault and battery in New York State. I once showed a series of paintings made under the influence of the Jewish concept of how the world, which is finite, can exist only if God, who is infinite, partially hides himself, and in the exhibition notes was a line from Proverbs: *It is the glory of God to conceal things, but the glory of kings is to search things out.* I liked the sound of this at the time, but I didn't foresee that people would think I was referring to myself: that I thought I was a concealing God or a seeking king or both. I was just talking about the mystery and how we approach it, either by dying or by the way we live. I wanted Darren to communicate with me every day because I wanted him to take himself seriously to the extent this was possible. I wanted him to have to notice that he was alive at least once a day. I saw now what Ana saw after the earthquake, that the game was already over. Every minute we got now was just extra time.

I'm still surprised you never got it that Leslie was pregnant that summer, Darren had written to me just before I drove to visit Jesse that morning. *I thought it seemed kind of obvious. I was thinking at work today about how when you found out we were having a baby, it made you handle things the way you did, or at least pushed you in that direction. That's what I was thinking about while I was prepping the counter with all the fucking fillings today, black beans and pinto beans, ground beef and chorizo and chicken tinga and regular chicken, I was really pretty stressed out that summer, trying to figure out life when*

I knew there was a baby coming. I couldn't picture it. I didn't know I'd be halfway across the country in Salt Lake City, hanging on by my fingernails, skating when I can skate because it's free, one of the only things that's free, once you have the board and I made that friend who hooked me up with that Element board. I would like to be sending Leslie money, I really would, but I know, I can already hear what you're saying, I'm just posing, fantasizing, I should remember how little I earn, stay within budget, don't make promises I can't keep, make them when I can keep them. Simple, simple, simple. Sometimes I just want to say fuck you, maybe you're right, but still, fuck you. Fuck you, Chris. How's it going? You sell that house yet?

Darren

I had written him back:

Doesn't sound like you made manager yet. How much extra is it for guacamole?

Be patient. That's something my friend in prison told me. I'm going to visit him right now actually, I just pulled into the lot.

Jesse sat by himself at a table by the wall wearing the jeans and white T-shirt of a convict, as he always said, not the street clothes he usually wore. The lighting was so bad I wasn't even sure it was him at first and when he stood up I realized I'd signaled this uncertainty. He had lost weight, his hair a little thin on top, gray strands in it, but his eyes were so clear that he looked younger than before—younger and older simultaneously, as if even the aging process got distorted by the climate of where he lived. The governor had still not signed his pardon recommendation, probably because he was up for reelection, but Jesse still had a year and a half to wait anyway. He asked how my drive had been and I told him fine and then I remembered his old-fashioned solicitude, which meant he wasn't just asking, he'd considered the risks of the long drive and was glad I'd made it safely. I told him I was going to meet Ana in a couple days in Texas, a state I'd never seen, and he told me the state of Texas always brought to mind the life he wanted to live when he got out of here—a pickup truck, football on TV, hunting or fishing on the weekend, a family maybe, but maybe not. Time was moving more and more slowly, he said. A month ago, he'd got locked up in a disciplinary cell for a fight that hadn't even happened. They released him three days later with no explanation but also no write-up, a mystery even deeper than being locked up in the first place. It was a way of reminding him that nothing was certain between now and when his chance for parole came up in a year and a half, he thought. It had been almost twenty-five years since he'd used drugs but the craving still came out of nowhere sometimes, as it did a few days after that, his chest tight, just waiting for the runny nose and the achy skin—it was a bad moment that lingered for a couple of days. He pushed his chair closer to mine and said he wanted to look at my healed eye. He'd been studying anatomy since the attack in my living room—he'd told me this before—and he put his fingertip on my eyebrow now and leaned in closer. There were six muscles in the eyelid, he said, just in the lid itself, not the eye, which had its own very complicated musculature. When you blinked, the six muscles in each eye kicked into action simultaneously. Flash. Twelve reflexes fired. Muscle tissue, nerve tissue. Microscopic tissue. The blade was like a backhoe cutting through all that delicate tissue, he said, all the way down to the level of the synapses.

"It's amazing it healed," I said.

He moved his chair back to the opposite side of the table.

"So you're leaving-leaving now," he said. "Sold the house. Quit the job."

"I should have left a long time ago."

"He's out there snowboarding or something now. Seeing his life coach."

"He doesn't have a life coach."

"Right. He has you."

"You sound like Ana. She was like that—upset about how I was dealing with it, how soft I was. She thought I was sentimental about Darren and his girlfriend and their baby, but I never felt anything like that when we were dealing with the possibility of having a baby of our own. She never said that exactly, but it's what I could feel."

"But you were being straight with her. You didn't want a kid."

"She didn't want one at first either. But I think what she sensed, and what I didn't sense, was that maybe we should try to have one anyway. She took me to that place outside

Guanajuato where the doctor was living with his perfect family, and even after she sat down and drew me that picture, I still didn't get it. There were these tests I didn't know I was taking, she didn't really know I was taking them either. It's not the end of the world. It's not the end of anything. It's just something we both know about each other now."

"So that's what you meant when you were saying you should have left a long time ago."

"It's easy to see it now. It would have seemed ridiculous two years ago."

He was involved with an old girlfriend from high school, he told me, a woman he hadn't seen or heard from in more than twenty years before she contacted him last fall. She'd started writing him letters, then emails, then talking to him on the phone and coming for visits. I knew from conversations we'd had in the past that people actually had sex in this visiting shed with its gray linoleum floor and stifled gray light that made it feel underwater. Sometimes they managed to do it right at the table with their clothes on, in front of the guards. There was a way to push the video games closer together to create a space that was hard to be seen in. That wasn't the kind of relationship Jesse described to me now, though. She was solid, he said, down to earth. She could talk to him about the most boring things—the people she worked with, how none of the stores carried her kind of cigarettes anymore, some lipstick she found that tasted like cake—and he would listen intently. When you compared it to how they fought, he said, it was like the sweet spot. Most of his life consisted of sleep, work call, eating, sleep—listening to her talk about some argument with her sister, finding a way to take her side and argue for it sincerely, was like getting high. She put money on his commissary and paid for his cell phone—that was how they talked and texted and even flirted with each other in public on Facebook. He knew that the asshole she was living with wasn't listening to her, he said, all that daily life shit. If he was honest about it, he admitted, he probably wouldn't listen to it either, if he was the other man. He knew this, but he couldn't really believe it because he was here, not there. It started to turn into this whole movie in his head—*Jesse and Antonia*—like he could hear the fucking soundtrack. I worried about the contraband cell phone but didn't say anything. The institution had special tablet computers that enabled you to check your prison email and download music files, which cost more than ordinary ones, and I had bought Jesse one of these players and funded it every once in a while, but now this seemed quaint, inadequate. He was having a love affair with a real woman who wanted him to have a phone and who, Jesse told me, got angry if he didn't stay in touch with it. He said the relationship was almost as much about arguing and strife as it was about happiness. They were drawn to each other but always forgot they tended to argue and look for ways to hurt each other. They must both get off on it, he said, laughing. He'd told her she had to leave the other man, it was untenable, he was going to cut it off with her if she didn't get her own apartment, but actually he was just like that other man, he said, all threats and no follow-through.

I went over to the booth out in the hall to order us some food. He got a double cheeseburger, a mammoth sandwich that dripped around his fingers and was hard to eat. I had a fish sandwich that was similar. The taste of the food, the difficulty of eating it, the solemnity of where we were, the fact that I'd paid—we were both trying not to think all these thoughts and both failing, thinking and eating in the silos of ourselves.

"Masochism," he said, shaking his head. "Is that what that is with me and her?"

"I think it's just ordinary drama. I had that kind of feeling with Malika sometimes."

"With Ana now."

"It's different."

"Different movie. Different soundtrack."

I sometimes felt that just because I was glad to be alive didn't mean I thought I deserved to be. Jesse's equanimity was something I could never fathom. When I used to try to imagine his daily life I would see gray dark hours or lurid violent ones instead of the textures and hues his eyes actually saw. I still couldn't see what he saw. I knew that. But what we could both see was an emptiness that threatened us and everyone else, the stupid void that Darren's box cutter came slashing through. I didn't believe that my arrangement with Darren was some small step toward making a better world. I knew that if I was serious about making a better world I would have to admit there was a war going on and step into the violence.

On the phone, Ana told me her brother Hernan had had a terrifying experience on a business trip in southern Mexico. A gunman opened fire in the restaurant while he ate dinner—people were shot and killed right in front of him. He was fine, she said, but the joke he made was that he felt like the saddest narco in the world there, sitting through a gun battle because he was considering investments in the cultivation of amaranth, a nutritious grain poised to become the next quinoa. She asked if I was all right, and I told her yes, I was glad I'd come here, it was good to see Jesse. She asked if I'd said hi for her, even though they'd never met or exchanged words, and I told her yes, though I hadn't.

"They're finally putting up my last podcast," she said. "The one about Parkland. I'm proud of that one."

"I'll listen to it later tonight. You have a good voice for podcasts."

"It was fine for a while. Whatever. I like what I'm doing now better."

"How is that kid now? In Parkland."

"Traumatized. Still. But when he talks he's calm, logical.

Like an adult. It's been a year and he still hasn't gone back to school. Maybe he'll go back next fall."

He was a Venezuelan immigrant whose family had moved to Florida, like Ana's had moved to Mexico City, to escape the collapse and find "a better life"—I don't mean to belittle that phrase but to amplify it. During the mass shooting, he was hit in the leg, but then he forced himself to stand up and close the door of the classroom, and in doing so got shot five more times. A teacher who tried to help him was shot in the head and killed right next to him. He went through thirteen surgeries. He saved maybe twenty people's lives by forcing himself to close the door. It reminded me of those boys being rescued from the cave in Thailand, the physical courage and also the thinking beyond despair—calm, logical, like an adult.

She told me she was leaving tomorrow for Juárez, then El Paso, where she was meeting a Mexican client to prepare for his trial. I asked if Juárez was really safe and she said it depended on which part of it you were talking about, her tone suggesting that this was obvious. I asked her how her mother was and she said status quo and I made a joke about how much I missed her—I didn't tell Ana I missed her because I didn't have to. She had seen what came out of me that night in my living room with Darren and had managed to move past it. It wasn't as simple as it sounds.

"Who's going to take care of that cat when you're gone?" I said.

"My mother will do it. I told her she had to pay attention to him at least half an hour every day."

"He's not going to like that."

"Estrella will take care of him too. She likes cats."

"I don't think that's really part of her job."

"My mother will deal with it. I think she kind of likes him too."

The cat was maybe close to a year old, Reynaldo, a stray we'd taken in. Unless you paid him a lot of attention, he charged around the house and broke fragile objects with his hind legs, whose length he couldn't gauge yet. He was already so big and svelte we called him the Clydesdale. We talked about Reynaldo for a few more minutes, then said goodbye.

I washed my face and sat on the motel bed in the dimness, the blinds closed. A part of me was so far from Mexico City that Ana and Reynaldo and everything we'd just talked about felt unreachable. There was the understanding that too many things were happening around the world all at once, all of them equally important, none of them visible inside the onrush. I shut my eyes and made myself concentrate on my breaths, counting to eight, then back to one, then back up to eight, watching the random patterns develop between my breaths and the space between the numbers, telling myself not to care about the patterns, reminding myself not to care. I did it with my eyes open then and it was like watching footage of myself in that room with the yellow bedspread, the digital TV with its channel guide and pizza delivery menu, the air conditioner's low revving, the desk with its shaded lamp and chair. If you looked at it all from the right distance, you saw how much skill and know-how went into every object, how highly evolved we'd become, humanity, remaking the whole physical world in our image.

19

Malika's grave was marked by a small white stone already tarnished with black mold. I hadn't been here since her funeral, it wasn't something I believed in, I thought, though I saw now that that just meant I hadn't wanted to think about what it meant to visit a grave at all. Across the street was a ragged playground hemmed in by wire fencing. In front of some of the graves people had set out bouquets of plastic flowers like petrified candy. Malika's stone had been chosen by her family, a part of her I never touched. She didn't feel shame about where she came from and she knew she belonged anywhere she wanted, everywhere she wanted, which was how I met her in New York, not here where she was born, this part of the world that was as foreign to me as Caracas or Guanajuato. She could be serious when we were alone but in front of others she hid behind a kind of belittling playfulness, as if everyone she knew including me understood she was a star, but she liked having people around, not in a patronizing way, I mean she savored her own attractiveness. Why does the eye strain toward the brightness, the spectrum, the signal, feeding on it like food, forgetting threat or shock, the inevitable fight or flight? It never made sense to me that we got along, we just kept getting along. Some people don't seem to feel much, and as a simple evolutionary device to help us survive, love seems more elaborate than necessary. When we first met she thought I was a Palestinian, and when she found out I was something else I could see her puzzlement, her face saying she didn't know something like that was even possible, but she stayed. I had wanted to stop wanting things before I met her, that was why my painting had started to fade out, because I didn't care about it to the necessary degree. There's no way to make art without someone telling you what's wrong with it, where and how it falls short, what that says about you, how and why it could be better if you were less blind, and only a fool spends time thinking about statements like that, about what other people think. But I fell into getting along with Malika in that time of wanting not to want. Maybe you have to be intoxicated in some way in order to live. I could feel her body underneath the ground. I could feel it was dead. I could feel her spirit spreading up and out over the cemetery's stones, the weeds, the playground's broken swings. I knew that healing could be painful. I thought I knew that, but really you just forget that it never stops.

I was taking my leave, not knowing when or if I would ever come back to this country. I needed some time to locate myself in time and space, but driving down that rural highway flanked by ditches through a landscape of gas stations, churches, dollar stores, and fast food places in the vaporous heat seemed like a dream of a memory, not something in front of my eyes. There was a detention center on the way back into town, a huge facility that I later learned housed more than a thousand asylum seekers who'd crossed the border from Mexico, incarcerated there for money in this place that had no industry, no farms, no jobs other than service jobs, now prison jobs. Meaninglessness, the failure to create meaning—I didn't believe there was such a thing as meaning, but I knew the active pursuit of it was sanity, and that the opposite of sanity was whiteness, death. I parked at the motel and walked briskly toward the air-conditioning inside. In my room, the blue peace behind my closed eyes settled in. Because I wasn't moving the lid, I didn't feel the itchiness of the scar and instead felt the comfort of my own private nothing or my private everything—I won't say it was nothing, it didn't feel that way to me.

20

It's been five months and I still haven't heard any-thing back from Diana, Darren wrote the next day. I assume you would have told me if she contacted you. How many times did you reach out to her? I can't apologize obviously to someone who won't let me get them a message even through a third party. But you know that, that's why you agreed to reach out to her. I assume you told her what I told you. That's all I really want to tell her, or just that I'm sorry. I didn't really think of it as pushing myself on her, though I know that's not the point. Not at all. It was like I was seeing through scratched plastic all that time. Like the plastic was actually stuck to the lenses of my eyes. Obviously it's going to hurt when you rip it off. The brightness.

Keep the shit job. Keep going to the meetings. Get myself enrolled in classes in August. I have to be honest with you, *it would be easier if Leslie and Diana or at least one of them would get in touch with me. Like I wasn't just this unskilled worker in Salt Lake City but an actual human being. I guess the answer for now is to just stop thinking about it. Try to. That's my big idea for the day. Try not to think about it.*

Darren

I met his father the week I sold my house, just before I flew south. I was packing up all that hadn't gone in the yard sale and taking it to the dump, when he pulled into the driveway, a dry blond man with a mustache and glasses and the square stance of someone who got the first punch in. I took him down to the dock where we had something to look at, the silver water, the bare trees gray and cinnamon in the cold afternoon light. He didn't understand why I hadn't put his son in prison. I could tell by the way he looked out at the pond that his feeling was not so much confusion as of being condescended to.

"I didn't see any sense in fucking him up more than he already was," I said. "I had a problematic life too for a long time. The only difference was I did things I could get away with. It ruled certain things out, like what happened here."

"There was never anything for him to do out here," he said. "There's the fishing business in the summer, tuna and shark trips, but in the winter there's nothing. That's where the drinking comes in, the drugs. It's not just Darren."

"He liked fishing, working on the boat. That's what he told me."

"He liked it as a thing, not as a job."

"It's not an easy job."

"I basically don't set foot on land for six months once the season starts. If I'm not doing two- or three-day trips out to the Canyon, I'm doing two charters every day, morning and night. I come in and maybe take a shower, hardly eat. Six months of that. It's the only way to make your money, you have those six months."

It was the day before the day I sat down in the realtor's office and went through the closing. It turned out that Darren's father played guitar at a monthly open jam session at a brewpub in the village, and there was a session that night that I went to with Jerome. This subculture of jazz players from all over the Island, all of them men, gathered in the pub that evening—men in dress slacks and office shirts, men in baseball jackets, an eccentric with a white beard and a special cloth glove for his fingering hand on the trumpet. They played with a higher level of skill than I would have expected, not just memorized riffs bolted together. Darren's father was intently serious, no expression on his face, his eyes fixed as if he were reading the music off a chart but he was actually just concentrating, he knew all the songs by heart. His big Gibson L-5 was cumbersome compared to rock guitars. He was always on the edge of not being able to play what he wanted to play fluently, but he got there. You saw when he finally soloed that he played the way a former rock guitar player would play, a virtuosity geek who grew out of that and took up jazz with the same commitment to proficient technique. I was watching him with Jerome, wondering how Jerome felt about all these white men playing this music originated by Black people, not knowing what to make of the contradiction before us as Darren's father moved skillfully up and down the fretboard in a precise emulation of George Benson or Grant Green. I was almost certain he had voted for the president, but now I had to face the problem that I would never know and he would never have to say.

Ana and I had some time to kill before our flight back to Mexico City. We'd met each other in El Paso, but there wasn't much we wanted to see there, and since our hotel was downtown, near the border, we walked across the bridge over the Rio Grande to Juárez. The river was low, its banks reinforced with concrete levees muraled with graffiti on the Mexico side, plain gray on the U.S. The pedestrian corridor had iron girders and steel mesh on the side facing the river, so you couldn't jump, the left-hand rail open to the roadway, a vaulted sunshade overhead the color of balsa wood. All the traffic moved in one direction, from Juárez to Texas. We walked up and showed our identification without standing in line, immediately feeling the difference in the countries, Mexican traffic different from American traffic, Mexican sidewalks different from American sidewalks. Just off the bridge someone was selling postcards and candy under an orange umbrella. We continued a long way down Avenida Benito Juárez until we finally came to the main square with its Scotiabank, its flavored ice vendors with their coolers on yellow bicycles, and at the far side, the cathedral with its twin bell towers. There were stalls shaded by white tents displaying girls' dresses, mezcal in ornamental bottles, toys, quinceañera gowns, then an arcaded plaza with a band shell in a shabby patch of greenery. Juárez—I couldn't connect all I'd heard about its violence to this placid scene, not even as a sense of ghostly absence. Ana hardly ever talked to me about her work, which often had to do with the most irrational, terrible forms of violence. All she said now was that her client's trial had been postponed, she'd have to come back to Texas in a few months. It was no easier to advocate for a man who had shot and killed someone for trying to steal the paycheck he had just cashed than it was for a man who'd murdered children, or twenty hospital patients over a period of years, drugging them while working as an orderly. It was bright and dusty in Juárez, the buildings made of white or gray or pink stone, ordinary families and old people out shopping, Ana and I the only ones in sight who weren't from here or at least from Mexico. There were department stores, fruit juices in eight different flavors in five-gallon plastic bottles. The advocacy Ana did wouldn't even get her clients out of prison, it would only spare them from the death penalty in a country that wasn't theirs. All I'm saying is that this city was known as one of the most violent places in the world and all these people were still here as they'd always been, black grime on the gray stones, tamarind juice, pineapple juice. No one looked at us except out of curiosity—strangers or tourists or whatever you wanted to call us, resident aliens—and even the curiosity didn't last very long.

"I just wanted say, I understand what you're up to with Darren," Ana told me. "It's just that I don't like him."

"It's not about liking."

"Principles. I used to think everyone should have strong principles. Ideals they were willing to stand up for, that kind of thing, but I don't know anymore. Maybe I'm too old to think like that anymore. But I guess I still think there's more to life than just, what, happiness. Happiness is good but it's not everything."

"It's better than unhappiness."

"It's one of those words that means less and less the more you think about it."

21

Our life in Coyoacán could be trying, more family time and less privacy than I liked, but I started to enjoy cooking with Ana's brother Hernan on weekends when we'd prepare large feasts with complicated dishes we were both just learning how to make. One of the most involved ones was chiles en nogada, which you ate only in the fall, when fresh walnuts came into season, their soft meat pureed with spices into a thick white sauce that you poured over stuffed poblano peppers and garnished with a sprinkle of bright red pomegranate seeds to make the colors of the Mexican flag. I'd started eating chicken stock and various kinds of meat, pork in this case, which Ana and Hernan insisted was raised in a more humane, less corporate way here than in the U.S., but I did it mostly because I was living inside their family now, which mattered to me more than I would have predicted, and even I admitted that it smelled good, tasted good. I had come away with a little money from the sale of my house on the Island, not a lot, but enough that Ana I and could start looking for a place of our own, though we would still spend some nights with Consuelo as part of a rotation with Hernan and his wife when Estrella had her days off. I was going to have my first painting show in almost fifteen years that September—it was in the gallery Ana and I had never managed to get inside when I first came here, the big one across the street from the café where we met after our breakup—and I was trying to produce some new pieces to go with the old ones I'd brought back from Lucien's place in New York. Ana came by my studio from her job one day after lunchtime so we could go look at a new apartment that happened to be just a few blocks away. The realtor had called to say the appointment was delayed, so I did a little more work while Ana sat on the couch, theatrical in her black jacket and white blouse, red slacks, her styled hair snaking down in front, reading glasses resting on top of her head, her phone on her thigh. I was bent over a canvas spread out on the floor with my brush dipped in a bucket of refined turpentine, varnish, and linseed stand oil, and she was telling me to just leave it the way it was, it was fine, but we'd had that kind of exchange enough times that she didn't expect me to even acknowledge it. The painting was glaring blues, reds, grays, made with sign painter's enamel smeared with a housepainter's brush over a base layer of roofing cement, a ground that never quite dried, creating volatility and useful accidents. I wouldn't have been able to do the real painting in front of Ana, it would have felt melodramatic, but I could perform this busywork with her there now because it was easy and because it had more to do with erasing something already there than creating something that wasn't. You just know how to do certain things. I didn't think I'd know how to make paintings anymore but I did. I could never see what should happen next to make the picture work, it was always just darkness in front of me, but that was how it advanced, light appearing slowly as I moved forward.

"I know you think you're making it better, but maybe you're just making it different," she said.

"I'll take different. It looks expensive now. Shiny."

"It'll be more expensive when it looks cheaper."

"That's the secret. That's what I'm trying for."

"But only if it looks cheap in the right way."

"It actually has to look expensive in the right way."

"You're not very good at being cynical. It's like you haven't had enough practice."

"I'd say I had a whole lifetime of practice."

"Yeah, but it's like nothing sank in. You were there and you got through it but it didn't change you. It's not a bad thing, it's fine. I'm not saying it's bad. I'm just saying I know why you're ruining that pretty painting and it's not because of money."

I had a different aura as an artist here, inflated, tinged

with a myth of reclusiveness, addiction, exile, and this added to my fear about making new work, but I really was painting for money, no matter what Ana said. If I was trying to say anything with it, then maybe it was just that we were still here, Ana and I. If you could afford to buy the painting, then buy it—maybe that was all a painting or any work of art could ever truthfully say.

The realtor called again and said she was still stuck in traffic but that the super of the building could let us in and show us the apartment if we couldn't wait any longer. She would meet us there as soon as she could. It was on Calle República de Uruguay. By the time we got there, the realtor was waiting in the shade across the street in front of a small business hotel, waving at us, a woman in her sixties with sunglasses on and the same kind of quilted black vest that Ana's mother, Consuelo, often wore. The walk from my studio had taken us past the Zócalo with its protesters under plastic tarps onto a stretch of crowded shoe stores and clothing stalls, a 7-Eleven, an old man in a wheelchair singing karaoke for change, and the turn onto Uruguay was no less congested and loud. The apartment building was sandwiched between two herbalist shops, marked by a huge wooden door that was at least a hundred years old, which was the first sign of what we eventually saw. As soon as we got inside that door and closed it, it was not only quiet but almost silent.

There was a car parked in the courtyard, a Renault sedan

from the '80s, and then a zigzag of narrow stone stairs that took us past a landing with a courtyard full of potted plants and a folk art statue of St. Francis, then another flight up to another landing, belonging to the apartment we were there to see, which had even more potted plants and which you entered through glass doors as into a greenhouse at a botanical garden. The stairs were as steep as the side of a pyramid and we were breathing heavily when the realtor opened the door to the main apartment—it opened right into the bedroom, a cool and shaded space mostly filled by a pale purple bed with a canopy that was just a suggestion of a canopy, simple high posts connected by crossbeams, all of it painted a deep blue that matched the blue of the walls and even the ceiling. The apartment had looked small on the internet, and it was small, but the ceilings were at least fifteen feet high with skylights beyond the old rough-hewn wooden beams, which made the rooms look bigger, though it was the blueness of the furnishings that made the overwhelming impression. We would obviously not be getting the furnishings but it was not hard to imagine replicating them or doing something similar. The walls in the other rooms were all covered with a kind of faux Victorian wallpaper with intricate horticultural patterns in lime green on white, or deep blue on white, except for one room, which was wainscotted in olive green and had huge built-in bookshelves on one whole side. The furniture was all the same deep blue, most of it covered in velvet—sofas and chairs and even a chaise longue, broken up with an assortment of side tables and dramatic lamps—living room, dining room, a small kitchen off the back stairs. It belonged to an interior designer, the realtor told us, he was moving to Mérida. There was another terrace off the dining room with some lounge chairs and a picnic table and a full miniature garden—potted trees, hedges, succulents, geraniums. We had looked at a lot of apartments in our price range all over the city. The only reason this one was affordable, the realtor explained, was it was on the wrong side of the Zócalo, but the neighborhood was changing, it wouldn't be affordable much longer.

"It's like being inside a houseboat," Ana said. "The light in here, it's like we're near the water."

I knew what she meant but what I felt was that it was like 1966 in there, an idealization of 1966, just the good drugs and clothes and not the police violence or the riots or the wars.

We walked back to my studio, the street life before us distant and glowing now that we were looking at it from within the daydream we were still having of the apartment. Ana connected her phone to my stereo and the first song in the shuffle was by a woman singer who reinvented old ranchera and norteño and cumbia sounds with one of the most expressive voices I'd heard in a while, pushing through irony into sincerity but then somehow getting back close to irony, then pushing through it again. I had ten paintings up on the walls, the abraded shapes and signs smudged over with dark resin to bend and shift whatever obvious messages were trying to transmit themselves through the storm of colors. The paintings didn't understand the music and the music didn't seem to notice the paintings at all. Ana's black jacket, her white blouse, her red pants cut straight and slim reminded me of a cadet, then of a bullfighter, while the singer sang in Spanish over a two-beat cumbia about shrugging off a skin she felt imprisoned in. It was Manet I was thinking about—Ana's clothes were like a Manet. We were sort of dancing and kissing but part of us was still in the apartment with its blue furniture and patterned wallpaper while another part of me was vividly unbuttoning Ana's blouse while her jacket was still on—black, white, red, then lace bra, beige skin, my hands on the curves above her hips, the feeling of warm life, muscle, flesh, fat. I had a fold-out couch but we didn't bother to make it into a bed, we just fucked on the corduroy cushions with most of our clothes still on, the new ruined painting spread out on the spattered floor beside a clutter of buckets, paints, solvents, brushes, the scarified coolness of the older paintings looking on like displaced people, coming to terms with the brightness of the cumbia. It was only recently that we'd started having sex again without the thought of trying to get pregnant. The Clomid treatment hadn't worked, not in nine months, and eventually she said it was a relief to stop trying, she was fine, and although I knew she felt we had a decent life, I wanted her to have what she wanted. I'd started wanting it too, or at least wanting it more than I thought I did.

She had an old boyfriend who'd loved the Rolling Stones, and one of their songs was playing when she came back with the key to the bathroom down the hall and the roll of paper towel. She sat with me on the couch then, her bare feet in my lap, holding a cup of tea I'd made for her. The song was about lying on the floor and doing a jigsaw puzzle on a rainy day while outside the world churned in its turmoil, which at the time seemed cataclysmic, unprecedented. The singer was just waiting patiently with his woman on the floor, trying to solve the puzzle before it started raining again.

> *Espero pacientemente*
> *Con mi mujer en el piso*
> *Resolvamos ese rompecabezas*
> *Antes que siga la lluvia*

The Spanish word for jigsaw puzzle was *rompecabezas*— head smashers, it meant literally. I liked the word *rompecabezas*. I wasn't great at languages but I was starting to feel better about my Spanish.

Coyoacán. We took walks all the time in the vast park called Viveros that was also the tree nursery for all the other green spaces in the city—alleys of pine, acacia, jacaranda, eucalyptus— turning down one of the side paths to see tai chi or karate classes, or school kids practicing for a play, or flocks of runners who took advantage of the circuitous clay paths, dressed in expensive gear, or competing in races on weekends with everyone in matching jerseys. Sometimes there would be someone showing off a pet macaw, or an iguana, or a boa constrictor, and Ana would always approach and hold out her finger before she even had time to think about it, it was just instinct, her hips moving forward, and when I recollected a moment like that later, I would occasionally take the next step and think of all the orphans in this world so young they never knew anything but abandonment, and I would weigh that picture against the darkness inside me, which I knew would never go away.

I found Consuelo alone in the living room that night. She and Ana had had a fight earlier about Estrella, whom Consuelo had accused of stealing, as she had before, a story we and maybe even Consuelo herself knew was not true. At her most difficult, Consuelo would look at me with a determined scrutiny, cold and strangely sexual, as if she was knowingly challenging Ana's place in my life, and she did this now in a long pajama shirt buttoned to the throat that fell to her calves, her gaunt face further narrowed by the severity of her haircut. I had to ascribe this confrontation to her illness but it was impossible not to feel it had a deeper history, hard not to think of it as part of her core.

"I know those people," she told me. "I used to live with someone like Estrella, I'm not ashamed to say that. You can't say the truth without people criticizing you now, but that's how they get away with things. They take advantage of guilt. It's fine to pretend we're all the same, but I know people like that. Ana doesn't know them."

"I'll talk to her," I said. "To Estrella."

"I don't think you know them either."

"'Them.'"

"*No bromees. No finjas.*"

"*No sé como bromear, Consuelo. No puedo bromear en español.*"

I was trying to say I wasn't lying to her, I wasn't trying to con her, but my bad Spanish had nothing to do with why I couldn't get this across. I couldn't get it across because although Consuelo was highly focused she couldn't see beyond the way she felt in this one moment, as opposed to the one before it or the one after. That made it hard to say if she suffered in her illness, if it was painful to be misunderstood when you never doubted you were right and everyone else was wrong, but I shouldn't say that. She didn't doubt herself but I didn't know how she felt later when she was in a different moment looking back on these feelings, or if she even could look back, and if you thought about it for a while either way was unbearable, though that didn't diminish my willingness to leave her alone that night.

Reynaldo had pissed all over our bed. The comforter had a special liner made of fabrics Ana had brought back from India, so it was meaningful to her. I could see this first from looking at Reynaldo, who sat with alert dignity on a chair, exuding impunity, and then from Ana, who was kneeling by our bathtub when she told me what happened, dabbing at the bedspread with a damp cloth, then running the cloth under the sputtering tap, then wringing it out carefully, then dabbing again. She was angry and didn't want me in there watching her, a little like whenever we were in my studio together. The studio gave me a private space she didn't have. I told her when we got the new apartment she could crash there by herself once in a while if she wanted and I would just sleep here. I knew Reynaldo's pissing on the bedspread hit her harder because of her argument with Consuelo.

"The apartment was small," she said. "The kitchen was really small."

"You'll never learn to cook in that kitchen."

"I'm never going to learn to cook anyway."

"It was nice, though. Obviously."

"We have to sleep on it."

"We can sleep on it, but I don't think it's going to change anything. Why don't you take that to the dry cleaner?"

"I don't even know if you can dry-clean something like this."

"They'll do it. They'll know how."

"You never had a cat, did you? The smell of cat piss. It never goes away."

She slept on her side facing me, her hands beneath the pillow, Reynaldo in the trough between us down by our feet. She made no noise as she breathed, her face serenely blank. Orwell said that by the age of fifty everyone had the face he deserved, but the same could be said about the faces of sleepers. I thought of the cave sculpture of Shiva in India that Ana had told me about that first summer we were together, the god's three aspects—creator, preserver, destroyer—rendered as three faces, the preserver's facing forward, the others' to either side. I'd seen images of it now. The face of the preserver was wisely still, his eyes shut, his pudgy closed lips at rest, not pursed or smiling or strained, and this was how Ana's lips looked now as she slept with a sheet, no bedspread, through a July night with a three-quarters-full moon. She had lashed out at Consuelo once for not knowing what the word *anthropocene* meant. *Antropoceno*: the geological period during which human actions are the dominant force shaping climate and the natural world. In a few days, she was going back to El Paso to advocate for a man who said he was innocent, though she didn't believe him, it was just that what he'd done was too terrible for him to make sense of or even acknowledge as real. He'd killed his girlfriend's six-month-old daughter when she left him to babysit so she could go to work. Ana never had a child and had embraced this work instead, which I occasionally thought had something to do with penance, maybe in relation to Venezuela, as if it wasn't just that she believed in helping to save her clients' lives, it was that she identified even with the guilty ones because she'd left her country behind as it died. There were other ways to look at it, I knew, more positive ways. I watched her sleeping face now, as still as the face of the preserver. I was tired but I stayed with it for a while. One way of looking at her work was that she was a hedonist and that it wasn't far from hedonism to compassion because both were generosity of spirit. She once told me I laughed in my sleep, which I had to believe though it didn't seem true. It seemed like something she would do, not me. It made me wonder what I could have been laughing about.

22

There was another mass shooting that weekend—twenty-three killed, twenty-three wounded—at a Walmart in El Paso near the airport where Ana had landed just the day before. The young man who'd shot up the church in Charleston, the young man who'd driven his car into the crowd in Charlottesville, now this young man whose terrorism had targeted Mexicans, or people he believed to be Mexican—this latest attack had the odd and lasting effect of making me feel that in some way I had contributed to it, even if this was illogical. I remember Ana staring at me through tears on a video call from her room at the same hotel in El Paso we'd stayed in together just a few months earlier. Imagine it, she seemed to say, and I kept dreaming about the bleeding that night alone in our part of the house as the hours passed. It must have been two or three

in the morning when I fell asleep in the chair. I would dream
it hadn't happened but was just about to. Then I would wake
up and it was like Ana and I were dying and just beginning to
realize it. She had driven by the Walmart the day before. She'd
been planning to stop there on her way home to buy a cheap
down comforter, because they were harder to find in Mexico and because our old one smelled like cat urine. When we
moved into the apartment on Calle Uruguay later that month,
it had the same quiet, somehow watery ambience, as if time
didn't exist, though time had already changed the way it felt
there. It felt almost like we were visiting, even when we started
to stay.

The morning of the attack, I fed Reynaldo and gave him some
fresh water, then I sat with him for a while while I drank my
coffee, jiggling a toy, watching him bat it out of the air with
a center fielder's dexterity, his white paws like gloves against
his mottled gray and black forelegs. I'd got a letter in the mail
the evening before, a surprise from Jesse's girlfriend Antonia,
who was not just his girlfriend anymore but his fiancée—she
had left the man she was living with and found a place of her
own in Beaumont, Texas, the state to which Ana had just returned for work. Inside the letter were two photographs of
Jesse and Antonia taken at the prison visiting shed. One was
a close-up of their entwined hands with matching rings on

their fingers, silver or maybe platinum, and the other was like an ad for an old sitcom, Antonia falling into Jesse's arms before a backdrop of a waterfall, perhaps Niagara Falls, both of them smiling into the camera. *455 days*, Antonia wrote in the letter. I didn't know if she was talking about Jesse's possible release date or their wedding day. It occurred to me that Ana had never seen a picture of Jesse—I had never taken one of him or of us together—and now, when she got back from her trip, she would see these photos and he would suddenly be a thousand times more real to her. I remember thinking about Ana and those photos that morning as I left to meet our friend Magdalena.

I took the metro all the way from Coyoacán to Magdalena's neighborhood in Condesa, imagining what this city would look like to Jesse, even just the subway with its orange cars, the gleaming marble floors of every station, the brightly colored icons for the stops—Insurgentes with its church bell, Sevilla with its aqueduct, Chapultepec with its giant grasshopper. Compared to New York's subway it was a miracle of cleanliness and speed, despite the density of the crowds. Ana had asked me to come with her on her trip but I wasn't interested in going back to the U.S., I told her, not until Jesse got out, I would go then, obviously, would be there to meet him outside the prison with Antonia and the rest of his family. Ana was having fantasies of finding some donor or philanthropic foundation to finance a different kind of work for her, advocacy for Mexican and Central American refugees seeking asylum, a job that would use the same skills she was using now but with less ambiguous goals, representing victims of violence instead of people charged with violent crimes. Before she went back to El Paso, she told me she sometimes agreed with the prosecution side, and that she was having a hard time right now remembering why she did this, building a case for mercy for people she wasn't sure deserved it, even if she believed in it in principle.

The shooter in El Paso looked different in every photograph, the kind of person you didn't notice or who couldn't quite prove his own physical existence. He got lost on his way to the Walmart that morning, then had something to eat in the parking lot, where a youth soccer team was holding a fundraiser. It was Saturday, which meant it was my turn to help Magdalena with her English (she helped me with my Spanish on Wednesdays). We met in our usual coffee place, which looked like Paris with its zinc counters, tiny white tables, bistro chairs with black caning. It was the kind of place that existed in any large city in the world, though that was not the side of the world the shooter had ever seen. I saw it so constantly that I often forgot it was just a side. Magdalena told me she was making a presentation in her formal English class next week about Ayurvedic medicine, which she practiced as a career, and she wanted to rehearse it with me now, using her laptop to show me the accompanying PowerPoint slides. She had her hair up in a messy bun and wore an old V-neck T-shirt that made her look like an art student, I thought for some reason, though she was as old as I was, long past her student days. Ayurveda was part of how she and Ana became friends, she told me, not because they shared an interest in it but because Magdalena and her husband, Esteban, used to spend time in Caracas, where for many years they'd been involved in an ashram. I didn't know there were ashrams in Caracas, I said, then immediately regretted the ignorance of this statement. I asked if it was still there and she said yes, though she and Esteban hadn't been able to visit it in a long time. They still sent money. It was a beautiful space, with a large Hindu-style temple, a dining hall and dormitory, two different kinds of mango trees that dropped their enormous fruits six months out of the year. You could stay there for free as long you wanted provided you helped with the cooking and cleaning.

"*Paraíso*," she told me. "I mean in the way of—spiritual, spirituality. It was not just a spa or *lo que sea*."

"Paradise in Caracas."

"I don't think it's what you imagine. You know, you laughed a lot there. That's the main idea, you have to learn how to laugh at yourself."

They were playing a song now by Chavela Vargas, a legendary singer with a husky alto voice of intense sadness who accepted that life burned and presented herself to the fire. Sometimes my life in Mexico didn't feel real, just as my past life in the U.S. seldom felt real anymore. Maybe today, I thought, it was the photos of Jessie and Antonia and those engagement rings that made my life here seem a little unreal. I was feeling distant, not sure why, as Magdalena went through her Power-Point presentation. It had something to do with that day, the inexplicable atmosphere. On any other day it would have struck me as charming how badly she wanted to say the word *throat* correctly, how completely illogical English turned out to be when you saw it through the eyes of a Spanish-speaker.

Imagine it, Ana's eyes would seem to say later on that video call from her hotel in El Paso, and I would picture her carrying a down comforter in one of those clear plastic bags with built-in handles, sunglasses on, as she stepped back out into the Walmart parking lot just as the shots started. There was more to what I imagined but I won't put it in words because words make images like that real. Something about the video feed distorted her face in a way that made her look more like her mother—the shape of her eyes, the bones in her nose—a resemblance I had never noticed before and would never stop noticing after that day.

I took the metro across town to the *centro* to get some work done in my studio. It must have been a little after eleven o'clock when I got to the Zócalo station—the news from El Paso would have broken by then, but I still hadn't heard it, even if I somehow sensed it. Loud drumming came from the cathedral across the Zócalo, where among the crowds and the police, men in Aztec dress—bare chests, war paint, plumed headdresses—enacted some mostly imaginary version of pre-Columbian rituals while others among them burned sage in iron pots and wafted the smoke over seekers who breathed in the healing vapors, not all of them tourists. I was walking in this kind of a haze down Calle Moneda with its street vendors selling socks and underwear and counterfeit Ray-Bans, then I turned back toward the Templo Mayor, the last ruins of the Aztec holy place whose stones had been used to build the cathedral. In my pocket I had a key ring decorated with thin silk ribbons in various colors, a souvenir from San Cristóbal de las Casas that Ana gave me when we first came here on which I kept my keys to the house in Coyoacán and to my studio, the keys to my new life. In the metro, I'd had a hard time getting my card to work at the turnstile. I'd placed it there and waited for the bar to turn, then jammed into it with my hip, then tried again, people pushing from behind, or moving reasonably through the lanes on either side of me. It was busy once I boarded the train, and it got more and more congested, so full by the second stop that I couldn't grab the handrail and had to concentrate to keep my footing. Eventually we were pressed against one another so tightly that when another person pushed his way aboard it knocked the wind out of me. I was supposed to transfer at Pino Suárez but I couldn't see the signs

in the car or the ones outside in the passing stations and I was
so distracted by then that I forgot if we'd gone three stops or
two, if I'd imagined the last one or failed to notice it. Balderas,
Salto del Agua, Isabel la Católica—I thought we were at the
Pino Suárez stop but I couldn't tell, so I decided to get off and
if necessary take the next train. I paused against the wall for
a moment, bent a little forward as the mob passed by. When I
finally reached my stop and climbed the exit stairs, there was a
huge diorama under plexiglass of Tenochtitlán, the Aztec city
destroyed by the Spanish, one of those historical displays you
pass by a hundred times without really looking at. I looked
at it then and it was as strange and familiar as my own life,
recognizable and incomprehensible at the same time.

Ana Ramirez—she had the most ordinary Spanish name
you could imagine, she told me when we first met, and I understood later that what she was really saying was I should
know the language. The drumming of the Aztec dancers had
stopped but I could still hear the eerie out-of-tune piping of an
organ grinder playing something far away that wasn't quite a
song. It reminded me of a trip Ana and I made a long time ago
to Xochimilco, the last living remnant of Tenochtitlán, which
like Venice used to be laid out not on streets but on canals.
There were boats for hire that had elaborately decorated signs
that the bargeman raised once you got out past the tunnels,
a kind of huge arching frame with the craft's name on it sur-
mounted by volutes and flags and animal faces and hearts, all

of it blocked out in bold colors, like those gardens that spell out words in different groupings of flowers. I bought Ana a cornmeal cake called a gordita from a woman on a wooden raft. It was not an arepa but it was warm and stuffed with cheese and Ana said it was just different enough from an arepa to make you remember one without missing it. Later, we came around a bend into a broader channel like a lagoon where there were many more boats, intersecting in their different colors at chaotic angles, the drivers all facing forward to avoid colliding, and in that thickening crowd you could find passengers from everywhere in the world—the three Americas, Europe, Asia, Africa—all those people like ghost images in my memory now, moving through water without thinking about much of anything except moving through water. She would never see Venezuela again, that was what she didn't want to say about the gordita. I could still remember the Island, where I'd lived, could picture it vividly—the light between the tree branches, the glow on the leaves—but none of it felt like it was there anymore. Everything had changed in such a short time. I came back into the moment now as I walked away from the Templo Mayor, the cathedral behind me, this monumental square of gray stone and volcanic rock the center of a universe of twenty million people, a chain of births and names stretching out endlessly behind each of them. I imagined a child whose face resembled neither Ana's nor mine, a stranger's face, the face of an orphan—for some reason I always pictured a daughter when I thought of us having children. Ana hadn't texted or called me all day and it would be another hour or so before she did. There were tourists in the security line beside the Palacio Nacional, a throng of people on the pavements selling shoes, baseball caps, wallets, popsicles, the vast unfamiliar city as timeless and doomed as everywhere I've ever been, the sun still shining down for now, second by second, minute by minute. I was thinking of this orphan's face I couldn't see. I turned off Calle Moneda onto the little street where my studio was, past the bike rack, the army surplus store, then I took my keys out of my pocket, standing outside the door to my destination.

Acknowledgments

A special thanks to Jami Attenberg and Garnette Cadogan, who saw this book through its many phases, and to Bill Clegg and Pat Strachan for their constant support over many years.

Thanks to Jameson Ellis, Elvira Zavala Guzmán, Alberto Barrera Tyska, Gabriela Alemán, Jim Brady, David Smilde, Alejandro Velasco for his book *Barrio Rising*, Eugene Constan, Edmund White, Yuri Herrera, Ladee Hubbard, Joshua Ferris, Tom Piazza, Maurice Carlos Ruffin, Susan Choi, Bernice McFadden, Daniel Castro, Peter Ho Davies, Simeon Marsalis, Deborah Luster, and Sarah Lazar.

© Sarah Lazar

ZACHARY LAZAR is the author of five previous books, including the novel *Sway*, the memoir *Evening's Empire: The Story of My Father's Murder*, and the novel *I Pity the Poor Immigrant*, which was a *New York Times* Notable Book of 2014. His last novel, *Vengeance*, was the 2019 selection for One Book One New Orleans. His honors include a Guggenheim Fellowship, a Hodder Fellowship from Princeton University, and the 2015 John Updike Award from the American Academy of Arts and Letters for "a writer in mid-career whose work has demonstrated consistent excellence." Lazar lives in New Orleans, where he is on the creative writing faculty at Tulane University.